THE IMMORTAL DUEL

Grayle and Falconer clashed first in the dark times before History began—and their meetings over the ages were the stuff of bloody legend. Now the climax to their long hatred was at hand—and they raced to meet at their final battle-ground . . . a rogue atomic power plant that menaced all of Earth!

"An exotic combination of myth and method makes for a fine thriller. . . . Very good!"

—*The Kirkus Service*

Books by KEITH LAUMER

Non-fiction

HOW TO DESIGN AND BUILD FLYING
MODELS

General Fiction

EMBASSY

Science Fiction

WORLDS OF THE IMPERIUM
ENVOY TO NEW WORLDS
A TRACE OF MEMORY
THE GREAT TIME MACHINE HOAX
A PLAGUE OF DEMONS
GALACTIC DIPLOMAT
THE OTHER SIDE OF TIME
THE TIME BENDER
RETIEF'S WAR
CATASTROPHE PLANET
EARTHBLOOD (with Rosel George Brown)
THE MONITORS
NINE BY LAUMER
GALACTIC ODYSSEY
THE DAY BEFORE FOREVER
PLANET RUN (with Gordon Dickson)
GREYLORN
ASSIGNMENT IN NOWHERE
RETIEF AND THE WARLORDS
IT'S A MAD, MAD, MAD GALAXY
RETIEF: AMBASSADOR TO SPACE
THE GLASS TREE
TIME TRAP

THE LONG TWILIGHT

KEITH LAUMER

A BERKLEY MEDALLION BOOK
PUBLISHED BY
BERKLEY PUBLISHING CORPORATION

THE LONG TWILIGHT

Prologue

Here in the darkness and the silence I dream of Ysar. In the mirror of my mind I see again her towers and minarets soaring in the eternal twilight of her yellow skies, casting long shadows across the lawns and pools and the tiled avenues where long ago victorious armies rode in processional under bright banners. Amber light glows on flowering trees and the carved facades of jeweled palaces. Once more in memory I hear the music of horns heralding the approach of triumphant princes.

I recall the voices and faces of men and women, of warriors and queens, of tradesmen and viceroys, of metal-workers and courtesans, of those who have lived and walked these streets, rested beside these pools and fountains, under the ocher light of the forever setting sun of Ysar. And I see the scarred unconquerable ships, proud remnants of a once great fleet, true to their ancient pledge, mounting on columns of fire, setting course outward to face the enemy once again.

Here in the darkness and the silence, I wait, and dream of Ysar the well beloved; and I vow that I will return to her, though it be at the end of time.

Chapter One

1

A man sat at a small desk beside an open window, writing with an old-fashioned steel-nib pen which he dipped at intervals into a pot of blue-black ink. A soft sea-wind moved the curtain, bringing an odor of salt and kelp. Far away, a bell chimed out the hour of six P.M.

The man wrote a line, crossed it out, sat looking across the view of lawns and gardens. His face was strong-featured, square-jawed. His gray hair lay close to a finely formed skull. His fingers were thick, square-tipped; powerful fingers.

"Writing pomes again, Mr. Grayle?" A voice spoke suddenly from the doorway behind the man. He turned with a faint smile.

"That's right, Ted." His voice was deep, soft, with a faint trace of accent.

"You like to write pomes, don't you, Mr. Grayle?" Ted grinned in mild conspiracy.

"Um-hum."

"Hey, game time, Mr. Grayle. Guess you maybe didn't hear the bell."

"I guess not, Ted." Grayle rose.

"Boy oh boy, the Blues are going to mop up on the Reds tonight, hey, Mr. Grayle?" Ted stood aside as Grayle stepped out into the wide, well-lit corridor.

"Sure we will, Ted."

They walked along the passage, where other men were emerging from rooms.

"Well, tonight's the night, eh, Mr. Grayle?" Ted said.

"Tonight?" Grayle inquired mildly.

"You know. The new power system goes on. Just pick it out of the air. Nifty, huh?"

"I didn't know."

"You don't read the papers much, do you, Mr. Grayle?"

"Not much, Ted."

"Boy oh boy." Ted waggled his head. "What will they come up with next?"

They crossed an airy court, passed through an arcade, and emerged onto a wide, grassy meadow. Men dressed in simple, well-made, one-piece garments, some bearing a red armband, others a blue, stood in groups talking, tossing a baseball back and forth.

"Go get 'em, Mr. Grayle," Ted said. "Show 'em the old stuff."

"That's right, Ted."

The man called Ted leaned against a column, arms folded, watched as Grayle walked across to join his team.

"Hey, that's the guy, hah?" A voice spoke beside Ted. He turned and gave an up-and-down frown to the young fellow who had come up beside him.

"What guy?"

"The mystery man. I been hearing about him. Nobody knows how long he's been here. I heard he killed a guy with an ax. He doesn't look like so much to me."

"Mr. Grayle is an all-right guy, greenhorn," Ted said. "That's a lot of jetwash about nobody knows how long he's been here. They got records. They know, O.K."

"How long you been here, Ted?"

"Me? Five years, why?"

"I talked to Stengel; he's been here nineteen years. He says the guy was here then."

"So?"

"He doesn't look old enough to be an old con."

"What's he supposed to look, old? So he's maybe thirty-give, maybe forty-five. So what?"

"I'm curious, is all."

"Hah," Ted said. "You college-trained guys. You got too many theories."

The young fellow shrugged. The two guards stood watching as the teams formed up for the nightly ball game played by the inmates of the Caine Island Federal Penitentiary.

2

It was a long, narrow room, dim, age-grimed, smelling of the spilled beers of generations. Weak late-afternoon sunshine filtered through the bleary plate-glass window where garish blue glow-letters spelled out FANGIO'S in reverse. A man with four chins and a bald skull bulked behind the bar, talking to a small, quick-eyed man who hunched on a stool next to a defunct jukebox loaded with curled records five years out of date. In the corner booth, a man with a badly scarred face sat talking to himself. He was dressed in an expensive gray suit which was dusty and stained. A gold watch gleamed on one wrist, visible under a black-edged cuff as he gesticulated.

"The bum is dough-heavy," the small man said, watching the lone drinker in the tarnished mirror through a gap in the clutter of blended-whiskey bottles on the backbar. "Did you eyeball that bundle?"

Fangio's eyes moved left, right, left as he scraped slops into a chipped plate.

"Seen Soup around?" he murmured.

The small man's eyelids flickered an affirmative.

Fangio laid the plate aside and wiped his hands on his vest.

"I got to go out back," he said. "Keep an eye on the place." He walked away, eased sideways through a narrow door. The small man went to the phone booth at the end of the bar and punched keys; he talked, watching the scarred man.

A woman came in through the black-glass doors. She was middle-aged, a trifle plump, heavily made up. She took a stool at the bar, looked around, and called, "O.K., snap it up. The lady's waiting."

The small man kicked open the door of the booth.

"Beat it, Wilma," he said in a low, urgent voice. "Fangio ain't in."

"What're you, the night watchman?"

"Go on, dust."

The woman twisted her mouth at him. "I'll get my own." She started around behind the bar. The small man jumped to her, caught her bracelet-heavy arm, twisted savagely. She yelped and kicked at him.

The doors banged as a squat man in a shapeless gray coverall came in. He stopped dead, looking at the two. He had a wide, dark face, bristly black hair; acne scars pitted his jaw and hairline.

"What the—" he started.

"Yeah, Soup," the small man said. "I was calling ya." He stepped clear of the woman, who snorted and yanked at her dress. The small man tipped his head, indicating the occupied booth.

Soup gave Wilma a deadly look. "Beat it," he said. She scuttled behind him and out the door.

In the booth, the scarred man was opening and closing his fist.

". . . golden bird of Ahuriel," he said. "Once flown, never to be recaptured . . ."

"What's he talking about?" Soup asked.

The small man shook his head. "He's scrambled." They

walked back, stopped beside the table. The scarred man ignored them.

"Try the left hip."

Soup reached out, with a practiced motion took the drunk's arm up behind him, forcing his face down onto the table. A glass fell over. Soup reached across behind the seated man, patted his back pocket, brought out a sheaf of currency, folded once across the middle. The bill on the outside was a fifty. Holding the owner's arm, he spread the bills.

"Hey," he said. "New shoes for baby."

He released the seated man's arm and stepped back. The victim sprawled, unmoving, with his cheek against the table.

They had taken two steps when the scarred man came up out of the booth in a lunge, locked his arm across the squat man's throat, and bent him backward.

"Stay, hagseed!" he hissed. His face was mottled, blurred, contorted. "Art *his* emissaries? Lurks *he* yonder?"

The small man made a grab for the money still in his partner's hand, missed, turned, and ran for the door.

"Find thy tongue, wretch, ere my dirk rips thy weasand!"

Soup's hand, clutching the money, waved near the scarred man's face; he plucked the bills away, as with a desperate plunge the squat man broke free.

"Stay, whelp, I'll have report o' thy master!" the scarred man snarled, making a grab at the man. He missed, staggered against a booth. The squat man disappeared via the rear door. The scarred man looked at the money in his hand as though noticing it for the first time.

"Nay . . . 'twere but a mere cutpurse," he muttered. "Naught more . . ." He looked around as the door opened cautiously. The woman called Wilma looked in, came through.

"Hey," she said. "What gives?"

The scarred man blinked at her, weaving.

"Fetch ale, wench," he muttered, and turned, half-fell into the nearest seat.

The rear door burst open; Fangio appeared, goggling.

"Hey, what—"

"Draw two," the woman barked. She sat down across from the scarred man, who was leaning back, eyes shut, mouth open. She stared curiously at his disfigurements.

"You know him?" Fangio asked tersely.

"Sure. Him and me are old pals." She transferred her gaze to the money in the drunken man's hand.

"Varför?" the scarred man mumbled. "Varför har du gjört det, du som var min vän och brör?"

"Why does he talk funny?" Fangio was frowning darkly.

"He's some kind of a Dane," the woman said quickly. "My first husband was a Dane. I heard plenty that kind of jabber."

"He looks like some kind of Jew," Fangio said.

"Get the beers," the woman said. "You ain't no Jew, are you, honey?" She patted the big-knuckled hand that lay on the table.

"Geez, will you look at them scars?" Fangio said.

"Used to be a fighter," the woman said. "What is this, a quiz show?"

" 'Twere but a dream," the scarred man said suddenly. He opened his eyes, looked vaguely at the woman.

"Just . . . dream," he said. "That's all. Bad dream. Forget it."

The woman patted his hand again. "Sure, honey. Forget it. Wilma will take care of you. Wilma's got a room, honey. We better get you there while you can still navigate. . . ."

3

At the Upper Pasmaquoddie Generating Station (Experimental), a dozen senators and representatives, the state governor, assorted lesser political lights, and a selected cadre of reporters were grouped around the Secretary of the Interior as he stood chatting with the chief engineer and his top aides before the forty-foot-wide, twelve-foot-high panel clustered thick with instrument dials and aflash with reassuring amber, red, and green lights, indicating that all was in readiness for the first commercial transmission of beamed power in the history of the Republic.

"It's impressive, Mr. Hunnicut," the Secretary said, nodding. "A great achievement."

"If it works," a saintly-looking senator said sharply.

"The technical people assure us that it will, Cy," the Secretary said tolerantly.

"I'm familiar with the inverse square law," the senator retorted. "You go pouring power out into the air, not one percent of it will get where it's supposed to go. It's a boondoggle! A waste of the taxpayers' money."

The chief engineer frowned as the reporters jotted briskly.

"Senator, I don't think you quite understand. We aren't broadcasting power, as you call it—not directly. We erect a carrier field—somewhat similiar to the transmission of a Three-V broadcast. When the field impinges on a demand point—an energy-consuming device, that is, of the type responsive to the signal—there's a return impulse—an echo—"

"The senator knows all that, Mr. Hunnicut," the Secretary said, smiling indulgently. "He's speaking for publication."

A man in an oil-spotted smock came up, showed the

chief engineer a clipboard. He nodded, looked at the clock on the antiseptically white wall.

"Two minutes to zero hour," the Secretary said. "Everything is still proceeding normally?"

"Yes, sir, Mr. Secretary," the technician said, then retreated under the blank look this netted him from the dignitary.

"All systems are functioning," Hunnicut said, making it official. "I see no reason that we shouldn't switch over on schedule."

"Think of it, gentlemen." The Secretary turned to the legislators, and, incidentally, to the reporters. "Raw power, torn from the heart of the atom, harnessed here, waiting the call that will send it pouring into the homes and factories of America—"

"At this point, we're only powering a few government-operated facilities and public-utilities systems," Hunnicut interjected. "It's still a pilot operation."

". . . freeing man from his age-old drudgery, ushering in a new era of self-realization and boundless promise—"

"Sixty seconds," a voice spoke sharply from a ceiling grill. "Automatic hold."

"Proceed," Hunnicut said.

In silence the men stood watching as the second hand of the big clock scythed away the final minute of an era.

4

The scarred man lay on his back on the narrow bed, sleeping with his mouth open. His face, in the slack repose of profound drunkenness, was a ravaged field where battles had been fought and lost, long ago.

The woman called Wilma stood beside the bed, watching him by the glow of a shadeless table lamp. She tensed as the light faltered, dimmed; shadows closed in on the shabby room; then the lamp winked back to full brightness. The woman let out the breath she had been holding, her momentary panic dissipating.

"Sure, it said on the tube about switching over onto the new radio power tonight," she murmured half-aloud. On the bed, the scarred man stiffened; he grimaced, moving his head from side to side. He groaned, sighed, grew still again.

Wilma leaned over him; her hands moved deftly, searching out his pockets. They were empty, but she found the roll of bills wadded under the folded blanket that served as pillow. As she withdrew it, she glanced at his face. His eyes were wide open, locked on hers.

"I . . . I was just fixing your pillers," she said.

He sat up with an abruptness that sent her stumbling away, clutching the money in her hand.

"I . . . was going to take care of it for you." Even in her own ears, her voice sounded as false as brass jewelry.

He looked away, shaking his head vaguely. Instantly, her boldness returned.

"Go on, go back to sleep, sleep it off," she said.

He threw aside the mottled blanket and came to his feet in a single motion. The woman made a show of recoiling from his nakedness.

"Lookit here, you!" she said. "I didn't come up here to—"

He went past her to the enameled sink hanging crookedly on the wall, sluiced his face with cold water, filled his mouth and spat, stared at himself in the discolored mirror. He picked up the smeared jelly glass from its clotted niche, but it shattered in his hand. He stared narrow-eyed at the cut on his palm, at the black-red droplets forming there. He made a strange sound deep in his throat, whirled to look around the room as if he had never seen it before.

"Xix," he said. "Where are you?"

Wilma made a move for the door, recoiled as he approached her. He reached out, with a precise motion plucked the money from her hand. He peeled off a ten-dollar bill, thrust it at her.

"You'd better go," he said.

"Yeah," she said. Something in his voice frightened her. "Sure, I was just looking in . . ."

After she had gone, he stood in the near-darkness, his head cocked as if listening to distant voices. He opened his cut hand, studied it. The wound was an almost invisible line. He brushed the congealed droplets away impatiently.

His clothes lay across the foot of the bed. He began to dress himself with swift, sure fingers.

5

In the prison dining hall, the guard Ted sat looking worriedly across the wide, softly lit room at the small corner table where, by long custom, Grayle dined alone. He had glanced that way a few moments after the lights had momentarily dimmed down, on an impulse to share the moment with the prisoner, grinning a satisfied grin that said, "See, we did it," but Grayle had been slumped back, gripping the chair arms, his usually impassive features set in a tight-mouthed grimace. This had given way to a look of utter bafflement. Now Grayle sat rigid, looking fixedly at nothing.

Ted rose and hurried across. Close, he saw the sweat beaded on the prisoner's face.

"Mr. Grayle—you O.K.?"

Grayle raised his head slowly.

"You sick, Mr. Grayle?" Ted persisted. "Should I call the doc?"

Grayle nodded curtly. "Yes," he said in a ragged voice. "Get him."

Ted fumbled for the communicator clipped to his belt.

Grayle put out a hand. "No," he said sharply. "Don't call. Go get him, Ted."

"Yeah, but—"

"Go and fetch him, Ted. Quieter that way," he added. "You understand."

"Uh, yeah, O.K., Mr. Grayle." Ted hurried away.

Grayle waited for a full minute; then he rose, lifted the table, spilling dishes to the floor. With a bellow that rang in the peaceful room like a lion's roar, he hurled the table from him, and leaping after it, began overturning the unoccupied tables left and right.

Giant trees stand in blue shadow against the wide sweep of the virgin snowfield. A heatless sun hangs almost unmoving in the ice-blue sky. A fitful wind drives plumes of ice crystals across the slope.

A man moves slowly across the white slope. He is tall, deep-chested, massive-shouldered, dressed in a form-fitting suit of a glossy blue-black material ornamented by bright bits of metal and enamel. There are raw burn scars on the right side of his jaw and neck, and his dark-red hair is singed at the temple. He staggers as he walks, making his way doggedly downslope.

He reaches the center of the snow-covered meadow, where a swift stream flows under a thin skim of ice. Kneeling, he drinks, swallows a pellet from a pouch at his waist before he goes on. At dusk he reaches the sea.

It is wide, blue-black, laced with the white foam of breakers; the rocky shore slopes steeply down to the watery edge. The wind blows an odor of iodine and salt spray into his face. When he wades out, the cold numbs his feet through the waterproof boots.

Small creatures dart in the shallows. In a tidal pool among the rocks, a fish flops in water too shallow for swimming. He picks it up, looks curiously at the small life squirming against his fingers as he carries it back down to the sea.

Darkness falls. The man makes camp by trampling a

21

hollow in the snow in the lee of a craggy boulder. He lies looking up at a sky strangely impoverished of stars. A glow grows in the east; a vivid orange disk appears, brightening to a pure white as it rises above the treetops. It is a dead world, fantastically cratered, hanging so close it seems to ride just above the distant mountain ridges. The man watches it for a long time before he falls asleep.

The surf murmurs; the wind makes soft sounds fluting among the rocks. There are other sounds, too; soft rustlings and scrapings, stealthy crunchings. . . .

He sits upright, and by the bright light of the full moon sees a giant, bearded figure robed in furs leaping down at him from the rock ledge above; he throws himself aside, feels a smashing blow against the side of his head that sends him hurtling headlong into emptiness.

Chapter Two

1

Aboard the thirty-five-foot cabin cruiser *Miss Behave,* one hundred and nine miles out of Port Royal bound for her home port at Miami, Mr. Charles D. Crassman; his wife, Elizabeth, and their twenty-four year-old daughter, Elaine, relaxed comfortably in the handsomely appointed cockpit, sipping iced Scotch and soda and watching the sunset across the scarlet water.

"Beautiful evening," Crassman said. "We're making time. I told you we were smart to make the run at night, miss the heat."

"Daddy, what's that?" Elaine was pointing off the port bow at a curiously regular-shaped cloud formation; a great purple-and-pink wedge, its apex touching the horizon, its top merging with the soft evening haze.

"Nothing," Crassman said easily. "Just clouds."

"Charles, I don't like the look of that," Mrs. Crassman said sharply. "It looks like one of those, what do they call them, tornadoes."

Crassman laughed. "That's out in Kansas they have tornadoes," he said, and took a sip of his drink. But his eyes lingered on the cloud.

"Go around it."

Crassman had been half-unconsciously easing the bow to starboard, away from the looming formation ahead; at his wife's words he swung the compass pointer squarely back to 220 degrees. "Just let me do the navigating, all right?"

"It's so big," Elaine said. "And it's close."

"Just an optical illusion." Crassman's eyes were on the compass. The needle was drifting past 220 degrees to 210 degrees. He corrected with the rudder. The engines' tone changed faintly, became more labored. A slight swell had appeared across the flat water; the bow cut through the low crests with a rhythmic sound. Frowning, Crassman passed the spindles of the big wheel from hand to hand, holding the bow on course. The chop was more pronounced now. The boat bucked ahead, cutting across the troughs and ridges of oily water.

"Charles, let's go back! I don't like the looks of this—"

"Quiet!" Crassman snapped. "I have my hands full running the boat right now!"

"Daddy—is anything wrong?"

"I don't know!"

"The cloud—it's moving! It's crossing in front of us!"

"It's not moving—we're drifting sideways. There's some sort of crazy crosscurrent running—"

"Charles—please! I want to go back!"

"Don't be ridiculous!" Crassman continued to fight the current; the big cloud, deep purple now and dead ahead, looked ominously close. It rose, spreading, like an inverted mountain in the sky. Crassman watched it drift across his bow, begin to slide off in a curve to starboard.

"It's coming closer! We'll run right into it!"

"Daddy, can't you steer away from it?"

"Well—I hate to waste time being nervous about a mere cloud formation," Crassman said, but he was quick to swing off to the south, away from the cloud. Now the bow tended to swing to starboard. Crassman felt the sweat popping out across his bald scalp. His lips were dry. A brisk, steady wind was blowing directly into his face.

Mrs. Crassman gave a muffled shriek. Crassman start-

ed, looked back at her; she was pointing astern. Crassman's heart took a painful plunge in his chest. The cloud
was dead astern, and clearly closer than it had been five
minutes earlier.

"It's gaining on us!"

Crassman put the throttle all the way over. The big
engines opened up to a deep-chested thrum of power;
the bow rose; spray whipped back across the big, sloping
windshield. Crassman looked back. The cloud clung
grimly astern. Off the starboard bow, the setting sun
was a red ball on the horizon, slowly drifting across
the boat's bows. Now it was dead ahead; now drifting off
to port, sliding back past the boat. A vast shadow lay over
the water off the port bow, coming closer. It swept over
the boat. Looking back into the sudden darkness, Crassman saw the cloud, now dull purplish-black, dense as
granite, half-filling the sky. And now, over the song of the
engines, another sound was audible: a vast, bass rumble,
like Niagara multiplied.

"Good God in heaven," Elaine said suddenly as the
boat emerged from the band of shadow into the red
sunlight. "What is it, Daddy?"

Mrs. Crassman wailed, began sobbing.

His face chalk-white, Crassman clung grimly to the
wheel, no longer looking back, listening to the swelling
thunder behind him.

2

The meteorologist on duty in the United States Weather
Satellite in Clark orbit twenty-two thousand miles above
the Atlantic had watched the anomalous formation for
half an hour on the big twelve-power screen before calling
it to the attention of his supervisor.

"Something kind of funny down there, Fred, just east
of the sunset line," he said, pointing out the tiny, blurred

disk hugging the sea to the west of Somerset Island in the Bermudas. "It formed up in a matter of a minute or two, smack in the middle of a twelve-hundred-mile-wide high that was clear as window glass. And it's growing steadily."

"An explosion, maybe?" the section chief suggested.

"That thing's over three miles wide already, Fred. It would take a nuclear blast to produce a smudge like that. Anyway, if it was a test shot, we'd have been notified."

"Maybe a nuclear ship blew her reactors. It's never happened before, but there's always a first time."

"The rate of dissipation's wrong for an explosion. It's not spreading fast enough. And I think it's rotating."

"Well, keep an eye on it, Bunny. Maybe you've nailed the first hurricane of the season."

"If so, I've got a lot of meteorology to unlearn. Check with Kennedy, will you, Fred? Something about that spot worries me."

A quarter of an hour later, Fred was back in the observer's bubble.

"Kennedy says no report of any detonation in the area. The autostations along the Atlantic seaboard are registering faint air-mass movements north and east. It's a little early to tell if there's any correction."

"Why doesn't it dissipate?" Bunny asked. "What's holding it?"

"Hard to say. Better put the recorders on it, Bunny. But don't worry; old Mother Nature is always springing surprises on us, just when we think we know it all."

Back in the communications center of the giant satellite, Fred flipped the key activating the beam linking the station to Kennedy Weather Control.

"Jake, no panic, but how about requesting an eyeball report on that fix I was talking to you about? The damned thing's still sitting out there like a tack in a board; and in the few minutes I was away, it grew visibly."

"Roger. I'll scramble one of the old Neptunes out of Jax. Those reserve boys like to joyride anyway."

"Keep me posted, Jake."

"Sure, Fred. Anything for our brave lads in the sky."

3

Twelve miles north of the village of Skime, Minnesota, Arne Burko, a seasonal trapper, threw down the armload of fallen branches he had gathered for his fire and seated himself on a log for a quiet smoke before dinner. It was a still evening, the sky tawny with the late-summer dusk. Burko lit up, stretching his legs, thinking of the forty-horse outboard on display at Winberg's in Skime. Everything a man wanted cost so much, seemed like. A car now. With a car, he could get into town more often, see more of Barby. . . .

He pushed away the thought of her warm body and smiling face. No point in getting all upset. He stood, paced up and down, sniffing the air. Off to the east, through the trees, the ground rose toward the rocky outcropping known locally as Vargot Hill. He hadn't been up there for years, not since he was a kid. Used to pick berries there. Supposed to be haunted, the hill was. Kids used to dare each other to go up to the top. They'd creep up on it through the trees, getting quieter the closer they got.

There were big rock slabs up there, sort of stacked, as if they'd been piled up there by a giant. The kids had had lots of stories about the hill. About the dwarfs and elves that lived down in the rocks, and would come out and eat a careless kid who stayed too long after sunset. And about the devil who took the form of a big black panther and ranged around the countryside, looking for souls.

Burko snorted a laugh and got busy with the fire. When it was going good, he stacked some stones around it and put on the frying pan. He unrolled the greased-paper-wrapped bacon, put half a dozen strips on. They'd be a little smoky with the green fire, but he didn't care. Walking all day made a man hungry.

Funny about that black-cat legend. Old man Olsen said the name "Vargot" was a corruption of an old word that meant "black cat." Probably went back to some Indian legend. The Shoshonu had been big storytellers. Big liars. Swedes were pretty good liars too, when it came to embroidering a tale. He'd made up his share. That one time, after he'd spent the best part of an afternoon up there playing on the rocks at the top of the hill, he'd been a short-term celebrity among the boys after he told them about the rock that had started to lift up while he was sitting on it, and how he'd had to weight down all he could to hold it in place. That one had held them with their mouths open until Fats Linder had said, "Nuts, Burko, nobody can weight down any harder than what they are!"

He turned the bacon, cut a couple of slices of bread. He soaked up the fat with the bread, forked the bacon onto it, then put the coffee jug on. He ate slowly, savoring every bite. It was almost full dark when he finished. A full moon was rising, glowing big and yellow in the east behind the hill. He banked the fire, stretched, then on impulse started up the slope, along a faint game trail, grinning a little at himself as he felt a ghostly touch of the old superstitious apprehension.

He made his way up through dense blackberry brambles, not yet in fruit, emerged onto the nearly level stretch just below the giant's castle. He had never really noticed it before, but the place had a sort of look, if you saw it in the right light, as if somebody *had* piled those rocks up there. Just nonsense, of course; the glaciers had dumped rocks all across this country; but these rocks were all of a size, pretty near—and they had a kind of quarried look about them. And the way they were arranged, sort of in a big rectangle, as far as you could tell for the growth. . . .

Burko froze, looking up at the looming pile. Had something moved up there, something that flowed from shadow to shadow . . . something that moved fast and smooth as a cat?

He was aware of his thudding pulse, of the tightness of his scalp.

"Hell." He laughed aloud. "I'm as bad as a kid. The thing's probably an Indian mound. Full of busted pots and arrowheads and maybe some skulls. Dead Indians. What the hell." He went forward with a bold stride, climbed up the slanting slabs, stepped up onto the flat stone that topped the structure. He was breathing hard, sweating lightly. A deerfly found him, buzzed his face sharply. He slapped at it. It was completely silent then. Burko took a step across the stone and halted. He stood that way for a full ten seconds, feeling his insides turn to water.

Unmistakably, through the stone he felt a faint vibration. Below his feet something ancient and evil was stirring. . . .

Arne Burko was over three miles from Vargot Hill when he stopped running. He had sprained an ankle jumping down the rock slabs but had failed to notice it at the time.

A week later, his throat was still sore from the yell he had uttered as he fled.

4

In the office of the governor, Caine Island Federal Penitentiary, the prison psychologist leaned forward across the desk, raising his voice over the shrill of the rising wind that buffeted outside the big, oak-paneled room.

"I think you're making a mistake, sir," he said. "The

man has a record of violence. He's dangerously un-stable—"

"Unstable, or unclassifiable, doctor?" The prison gover-nor cut in.

"I admit the man's an enigma," the psychologist said. "I don't pretend to understand his motivations. But after this outburst, anything could happen."

The governor turned to stare out the high windows behind his desk. The low sky, clear an hour before, now shed a light the color of dishwater across frond-strewn grounds, reflected from the whitecapped, hammered-pewter sea beyond. Through the massive leather chair and the deep pile carpet the minute trembling of the steel-and-concrete building was plainly detectable. As the governor watched, a forty-foot royal palm, curved into an arc like a strung bow, snapped, fell across the massed bougainvillea that lined the south drainage canal.

"No one was hurt, I understand," the governor said.

"No; but, Governor, you should have seen what he did to those chairs. Steel tubing, mind you. He twisted them into chrome-plated pretzels! Talk about maniacal strength—"

"Where was his guard?"

"He played sick, sent him for the duty physician."

"Got him safely out of the way, in other words."

"Governor—aren't you finding excuses for this man?"

"There was a reason for the outburst, as you put it, Claude," the governor said. "I want to know what that reason was."

"Governor, this is an old con, a man who once took an ax to a human being. In this day and age, an *ax,* for God's sake! The savagery of it—"

"Thank you for your opinion, doctor; your warning is a matter of record, in the event he tears my head off with his bare hands."

"I wasn't thinking solely of my reputation, Governor."

"Of course not, Claude. Nevertheless, I'm going to talk to him." The governor nodded to the uniformed man posted beside the armored door. The guard touched a wall plate; there was the soft double *click-click!* as the interlocks disengaged. The door slid back; the guard took up his position, choke gun in hand, watching as Grayle came past him into the room.

The tailored prison uniform accentuated his powerful physique. As the prisoner advanced across the room, the words "caged tiger" popped into the governor's mind.

"That's all, doctor," he said. "Guard, wait outside."

"Now, just a minute," the psychologist started. He caught the look his superior directed at him and left silently. The sliding door snicked shut behind the guard.

"Hello, Grayle," the governor said.

"Hello, Hardman," the prisoner said in a tone of absolute neutrality.

The governor motioned to the chair beside the standing man. "Sit down," he said. Grayle didn't move.

"Why?" the governor said. "Just tell me why, that's all."

Grayle's head shook almost imperceptibly.

"You knew I was working on a special parole for you. I'd have gotten it, too. So you picked this time to break up the dining hall. Why, Grayle?"

"You were wrong about me, Governor," Grayle said without expression.

"Nonsense, if you started smashing chairs, you had a reason."

Grayle said nothing.

"What are you trying to prove?" the governor said harshly. "That you're still a tough guy?"

"That's it," Grayle said.

The governor shook his head. "You're no brainless hoodlum. You had a reason—a good reason. I want to know what it was."

The wind shrieked in the lengthening silence.

"You cost the federal government over a thousand dollars in smashed furniture this evening," Hardman said sharply. "You've given the press new ammunition for their charges of coddling and lax administration."

"I'm sorry about that part," Grayle said.

"When you ran amok, you knew the effect it would have. You knew it would hurt yourself, me, the entire prison system."

Grayle said nothing.

"You realize what you're asking for?" A harsh note rang in the official's voice.

For an instant Grayle's eyes locked with Hardman's; there seemed to be some message there, almost readable. Then the prisoner glanced away indifferently.

"I'm ordering you to the maximum-security detachment at Gull Key, Grayle."

Grayle nodded, almost impatiently, the governor thought.

"I don't like it," he said. "I don't like to admit failure with a man; but the best interests of Caine Island come first."

"Certainly, Governor," Grayle said softly. "I understand."

"Damn it, man, I'm not apologizing! I'm doing my duty, nothing more!" The governor put his hand under the edge of the desk, touched something hidden there.

"I've switched off the recording system," he said swiftly. "Speak up now, man! Tell me what this is all about!"

"Better switch it back on. You'll have the guards breaking the door down."

"Talk, man! Gull Key is no picnic ground!"

"That's all I have to say, Governor. You're wasting your time."

Hardman's face flushed. He keyed a button on the desktop viciously.

"All right, Grayle," he said flatly as the door slid back and the guard entered alertly. "That's all. You can go now."

Grayle walked out of the room without a backward glance.

From a town of wood and stone houses clustered among giant trees and spilling down along the shore, men and women run down to gather on the beach; many of them wade out waist-deep in the bitter water to lay hands on the boat, shouting their greetings to the returned wayfarers. The prisoner climbs over the side with the others, grasps a rope, helps draw the ship up on the strand. Standing by the bow, he watches as the men caper, embracing the thick-bodied, snub-nosed women whose yellow hair hangs in thick braids down their backs. One or two of the latter eye him curiously, but they do not speak.

"Stand forth, slave," a deep voice booms out. A man comes toward him, a length of rope in his hands. He is tall, massive, with a tangled blond beard and shaggy hair, clad in garments of leather. Against his chest, the Star of Deneb and the golden Cross of Omrian glint among the polished bears' teeth strung on a rawhide thong. "It's time to truss and brand the bull for market, before he gets loose among the cows!" he shouts cheerfully.

The captive moves a step sideways, putting his back against the planked hull.

"Come and get me, Olove Brassbeard," he calls awkwardly in the language of the barbarians.

Olove motions with his free hand. "Bor! Grendel! Seize me that slave!"

Two big men come forward, smiling large smiles through bushy beards.

"It might be good sport to see Olove bind me with his own hands," the captive says. Bor hesitates.

"If he can," the slave adds.

Grendel's grin widens. He spits on the rocky ground. "The sea-law doesn't run here ashore, Olove. The voyage is over. You hold a rope in your hands, bind him with it —if you dare."

"You expect me, a chieftain, to soil my hands on a slave?"

"How say you, outlander?" Grendel inquires. "Were you a man of rank in your own town?"

"I was a Captain-Lieutenant." The prisoner gives the title in his own tongue.

"He lies," Olove blusters. "He was alone, without retainers or men-at-arms, clad only in a poor rag—"

"He wore ornaments of gold," Hulf says, enjoying himself. "The same ones we now see winking among the fleas on your chest."

"No doubt he stole them from his master ere he fled," Olove grunts.

"His ring fit uncommon well for a stolen one," Hulf says. "You had to hew away the finger to take it."

Brassbeard makes sputtering sounds; then he snorts and throws aside his wolfskin cloak. He flexes his arms, spits, and charges, his thick, bowed legs pumping liks pistons. The captive stands unmoving. As Brassbeard closes, he pivots minutely, elevates his left forearm to deflect the chieftain's outstretched hand, leans in to place his elbow in the path of the man's onrushing chin, swings with his rush to palm him on his way. Olove strikes the side of the ship full on, skids along it, to fall with his face in the water, and lie, his hairy legs twitching before they fall still. A roar of laughter goes up.

Grendel comes forward and rolls the fallen man over.

"Olove is dead," he says, still grinning. "He dashed out his brains on his ship to oblige the stranger." He wipes tears of mirth from his eyes, turns to the former slave, puts out a hand, clasps him below the elbow.

"The gods declare you to be a freeman," he says. "By what name do your friends call you?"

"Gralgrathor," the man says.

"Welcome to Björnholm, Grall Grathor. Come, my wife will find food and a pallet for you, and we'll share a flask or two. And for amusement," he adds in a lower tone, "you may teach me the spell you used to turn Olove's wrath into a madness that destroyed him."

Chapter Three

1

George, the night man at Smitty's Conditioning Parlor and Health Club, laid aside his paper as the buzzer sounded and feet descended the short flight of steps from street level. A tall, quick-moving man with a badly scarred face came into the room pulling off his coat.

"Yessir," George said, coming to his feet in a quick motion for all of his two hundred and ninety pounds of bulk, smiling, sizing up the newcomer. He noted the soiled cuffs, the wilted and grimed collar, the tear in the dusty knee of the trousers. But the suit was cut from a good grade of worsted, real wool, it looked like, and the big brogans were almost new under the dust and scuff marks. And the socks were a tasteful solid, none of those purple clocks. The guy had been out on the tiles, all right, but there was some quality there; he was no bindle-stiff just drifting in out of the damp night air. George caught the jacket as the man tossed it aside.

"Sponge and press the suit, sir?" he said. "Do it for you nice, while you're in the steam."

"Never mind that," the big man said. The scars on his face moved as he spoke, the big one across the cheek dimpling as if in a puckish smile, the one crossing his forehead and running back into the scalp lifting quizzically, sardonically. He shucked bills from a folded sheaf, tossed them on the table.

"My body's full of poison," he said. "I want heat. Lots of heat."

An elderly man, naked and shrunken, emerging from the infrared room, jerked his head sharply at sight of the newcomer. He halted, watching the scarred man strip. He seemed fascinated by the scars, large and small, that marked the powerfully muscled chest, back, thighs.

"I'm carrying one-twenty in the wet room, one-eighty in the sauna," George said. "Five minutes of that be all you can take."

"Call me in ten."

George watched the glass door, smiling a little to himself. He folded some towels, opened and shelved a carton of soap. Ten minutes, the man say. Like to see the man could take ten on them hot teak boards. First couple minutes go easy; then it start to get hot. Ten minutes. George chuckled. Door be opening any minute now. Big man be out, gasping like a catfish on the bank. He looked at the clock. Five minutes almost up. Through the clear glass he saw the scarred man sitting bolt upright, swinging his arms. Hoo-ee! That white man crazy, have to watch him, get him out when he faint. . . .

"That fellow's asking for a heart attack," the old man spoke suddenly beside George. He had come up silently, rubber-sandaled. He ruffled his wispy hair with a towel. "What was that he said about poison?"

"Booze, doctor," George said. "He meant the booze. Smell it on him."

It was eleven minutes before the scarred man strode from the dry-heat room, his body pouring with sweat. A sickly odor of alcohol hung thick about him. George stared.

"Cold water?" the big man said curtly.

"Deluge showers, right to your right." George pointed.

"Good way to get yourself a coronary attack," the old fellow called after him.

The scarred man stood in the stall, dousing himself with icy water. He breathed in great, shuddering gulps. Afterward he spent ten minutes in the steam room, ten more in the sauna, showered again. By then the reek of raw alcohol had dissipated.

"You know massage?" he asked George. George's wide black face crinkled in a smile.

"Some say I do pretty good." He nodded toward the padded table. The scarred man waved aside the proffered towel, stretched out face down. His back was solidly muscled about the shoulders, tapering sharply to a lean, hard waist. A deep scar ran down across the left trapezius to end near the spine. Lesser scars—lines, pocks, zigzags— were scattered over his hide in random distribution. Under George's hands, the flesh felt hard, ropy.

"You ever in the ring?" the masseur inquired.

"Not much."

"That fight racket no life for a man."

"Harder," the scarred man said. "I want to feel it."

"Got to be careful," George chuckled. "Man come home with bruises, his sweety wonder why."

"Say," the old man said. "Mind if I ask how you got the scars?"

The big man turned his head to look at him.

"I'm a doctor, a medical doctor," the old fellow said. "I've never seen anything quite like the way you're marked up."

"I got them in the wars," the big man said. George shot the oldster a pursed-mouth look.

"Don't shush me, George," the old man said. "My interest's legitimate."

"Got a little rheumatism there?" George asked. His hard, pink-palmed hands explored a lump under the client's skin. The elderly medical man came over, frowned knowingly down at the man stretched on the table.

"Be careful George," he ordered. "You take it easy

with those hands of yours." He leaned for a closer look at the deep fissure, keloid-ridged, that crossed the kidney region.

"Feel like some kind of lump there," George said. "Feel hot, too." He stepped back, looking at the doctor. The old man's thin fingers ran over the visible swelling at the lower edge of the prone man's ribs.

"Why, there's a bullet lodged in there," he said. "You been shot, mister?"

"Not recently."

"Hmmm. Must have entered along here. . . ." The thin old finger traced up along the big man's side. "Right here," he said. "Here's your point of entry. Traveled right along the rib cage—"

The medical man broke off, staring at an angry, reddish swelling developing at the spot under which the bullet lay.

"George, what did you do, gouge in with those big thumbs of yours? I told you to take it easy!"

"I never bear down on that place, doctor. I feel it right away and take it real gentle."

"You lie easy, mister," the doctor said. "You have some infection there, that's pretty plain. I have my kit with me. I think I'd better give you a hypo of PN-43—"

"No," the big man said. He was gritting his teeth, his back tensed. "I know what it is. But I'd forgotten how it feels. . . ."

As the doctor and the masseur watched, the contusion grew, flushing dusky purple now, a three-inch splotch against the tan skin. A patch of paleness grew at its center, spread to the size of a steel dollar.

"Hey, doctor—" George said, and broke off as the swelling burst, the skin splitting to ooze dark blood and clear matter, exposing a grayish lump. The doctor uttered an exclamation, scuttled across to an open locker, jerked out a green-plastic intrument case, opened it on a bench, hurried back. With a shallow, spoon-shaped probe, he levered at the wound, lifted out a slightly misshapen lump of lead as big as the end of his thumb. The big man sighed harshly and relaxed.

"How long ago did you say it was you were shot?" the doctor asked in a strained voice, eying the big slug lying on his palm.

"Quite a while."

"I should say so." The old man barked a short laugh. "If it weren't so ridiculous, I'd swear that was a genuine minié ball."

"Minié ball? What that?" George asked; his eyes rolled like a horse smelling smoke.

"That's what they used in the Civil War," the doctor said.

The scarred man smiled slightly. "I need food," he said as he pulled on his shirt. "Is there a restaurant nearby that you can recommend, George?"

"Happen I got a nice slab of sirloin in my cooler right this minute," the big black man said. "And eggs, too. About half a dozen sound right?"

The scarred man took the fold of bills from his pocket and shucked off a fifty, laid it on the rubbing table.

"Rare. And over lightly."

"Say," the doctor said. "Funny thing. The scars on your face: they look different."

The scarred man turned to the full-length wall mirror. He went close, studying his features. The furrow across his cheeks that had pulled his mouth into a perpetual faint grin had faded to a shallow, pinkish line. The broad band of lumped scar tissue across his forehead was now no more than a faint discontinuity in the smooth tan of his skin.

"Never saw anything like it," the old man said in tones of wonderment. "Those scars are fading right out. Just disappearing. . . ." His hand moved, caught itself. "You'll pardon my curiosity," he said, edging around for a better view. "But as a man of science—"

"They weren't as bad as they looked," the formerly scarred man said shortly, turning away.

"Look here, my friend, I'm Dr. Henry Cripps. Hank, to my friends. Now, I've had some experience with contusions and the like during over forty years of practice. I know a third-degree scar when I see one. A thing like that doesn't just disappear in the space of a quarter of an hour—"

"Doctor, I'm not in need of medical attention, thank you anyway," the big man said. The oldster clamped his jaw, retired to the far side of the room, from where he stared at the object of his professional curiosity. An odor of cookery wafted into the room through the open doorway to a back room. The big man paced up and down, flexing his arms.

"Itches, doesn't it?" Cripps spoke up.

"A little."

"Damnedest thing I ever saw."

Five minutes of silence ensued. George appeared at the door.

"On the table," he said. The big man followed him back to the small, neatly arranged living quarters. He seated himself and attacked the thirty-two-ounce steak. George put a big glass of milk in front of him. He drained it, asked for a refill. He ate the eggs, mopped the juices from the plate with a scrap of toast. George brought in a foot-wide pie, lifted a quarter of it onto a plate, put a half-pint mug of coffee beside it.

"Can't get that kind in the store," he said. "I got a lady friend brings them around." He watched as his guest finished off the dessert, drained the cup.

"Better hang on to that lady friend, George," the big man said. He rose. "Thanks. I needed that."

"I reckon," George agreed. "Too bad Lucy-Ann not here to see you tuck it in. Do her heart good to see a man eat."

"By God," Dr. Cripps said. "Will you look at that, George? You can scarcely see where the scars were. They're remitting completely."

George shook his head, accepting the evidence of his eyes philosophically.

"Nothing like a good feed to set a man up," he commented.

"Look here," Cripps said as the object of the discussion headed from the room. "Would you mind just letting me have a look at your back?"

"I'm sorry; I'm in a hurry."

"But damn it, this is medical history in the making—if you'd let me observe it! I have a camera in my apartment, a few blocks from here; I should photograph this, document it—"

"Sorry." The big man picked up his coat.

"At least let me examine the wound I dressed. You owe me that much."

"All right." The big man stripped off his shirt. The doctor's eyes goggled at the sight of the wide, unmarked back. He put out a hand, touched the smooth skin. There was no trace of any injury anywhere in the patient's skin.

"Sir," he said in a choked voice, "you must come along with me to St. John's Hospital. You must allow this to be studied by competent authorities—"

The big man shook his head. "Out of the question." He donned his shirt, tied his tie, pulled on his coat. He put another fifty-dollar bill on the table.

"Thanks, to both of you," he said. "I hope that will cover your fee, doctor."

"Never mind my fee—"

"It's late," the big man said gently. "Maybe you were imagining things."

"George, you saw it too," Cripps exclaimed, turning to the Negro.

"Doctor, seem like sometimes I got a powerful bad memory." George smiled dreamily, looking at the bill.

They watched in silence as the big man went up the steps.

"Where can I reach you?" Cripps called as he put a hand on the door. "I'll want to follow up on treatment, of course!"

The big man paused, turned his head slowly, as if listening for a distant sound. He pointed in a direction at an angle to the door.

"I'm going that way," he said. "I don't know how far." The shrill of the wind as he pushed open the door drowned the doctor's reply.

2

Four guards carrying choke guns and sidearmed with holstered 4-mm. impact pistols escorted Grayle along the wide, brilliantly lit subterranean corridor, two in advance, two behind him. In the liftcar, they posted themselves in the four corners and sealed their helmet visors before closing the door. In silence, they dropped the hundred and fifty feet to the staging room that was the sole exit route from the prison proper. As they emerged from the shaft, Ted was waiting. He stepped forward hesitantly.

"Hey, Mr. Grayle," he said in strained greeting.

"Hello, Ted," Grayle said.

"Uh—you O.K. now?" Ted said, and blushed.

"Sure. Thanks for everything, Ted."

"Geez, Mr. Grayle ..." Ted swallowed and turned away quickly.

"So long, Ted," Grayle said.

In the processing unit, Grayle moved stolidly through the chemical and radiation scanners, submitted to the cold caress of the medical unit, the icy touch of the hypo-sprays. His fingerprints and retinal and dental patterns were read and compared. A husky lieutenant flicked keys on the ID panel and recorded the response which certified the identity of prisoner 7654-K-3YN-003. He opened a steel drawer, withdrew a pair of inch-wide metal-link wrist irons linked by a ten-inch rod. He weighed them on his palm, looking at Grayle.

"I don't want any trouble out of you now, boy," he said. His voice was a casual drawl, but his eyes were sharp on Grayle's. He advanced briskly, snapped a steel ring in place on the prisoner's right wrist, reached for the left. He gripped it, then suddenly twisted Grayle's arm behind him, brought it to within an inch of the waiting cuff, then stopped. His face darkened; veins stood out on his forehead, but the cuff moved no closer.

"Do you want to call for help?" Grayle asked softly, "or stick to the book?"

"Don't get me mad, boy," the lieutenant hissed. "I've got friends at Gull."

"What do you do when you're mad, Harmon, blow bubbles?"

The man made a noise deep in his throat. "A guardhouse lawyer," he grunted. Five seconds passed in silence; then the lieutenant stepped back.

"I guess I'll give him a break," he said loudly to the sergeant. "This boy won't give us any trouble. He's got enough trouble. He'll want to hit Gull clean—as clean as his kind can be. Cuff him up in front."

The sergeant secured the manacles. The four armed men boxed the prisoner. Metal clanged as steel doors opened on a bare chamber. They walked in. The doors closed. Two of the men pushed buttons at opposite ends of the small room. A heavy panel slid aside on a big bright-lit garage where two massive gray-painted vehicles bearing the letters CIFP were parked. An attendant unlocked a door at the rear of one; one of the guards stepped up into the windowless compartment, covered

Grayle as he entered. A second guard came aboard, and the door closed. Locks snicked.

"You sit there." The guard indicated a low bench with a sloping back mounted against the driver's compartment. When Grayle was seated in it, knees high, his weight on the end of his spine, a locking bar slid into place across his ribs and sealed with a click. The two guards strapped into the contoured chairs mounted at the sides of the car. Each pressed a button set in the armrest of his chair.

"In position," one said. Grayle heard a soft sound, saw a minute movement of the tiny glass prism set in the ceiling. It studied him, then swiveled to inspect the guards. The light died behind it. A moment later the turbines started up with a muted howl.

Grayle felt the car move forward; he sensed the raising of the flint-steel door, was aware of a sense of enclosure as the vehicle entered the upward-slanting tunnel.

One of the guards stirred in his seat. He was a young fellow, with a bone-and-leather face, prominent teeth.

"Just try something, bo," he said in a husky whisper. "I hear you're a tough boy. Let's see can you break from us."

"Shut up, Jimbo," the other man said. "He ain't going noplace."

"Just to Gull, is all," Jimbo said. He smiled, exposing untended molars. "You think he'll like it there, Randy?"

"Sure," Randy said. "His kind likes it tough."

Grayle ignored their conversation. He was listening to the muted, echoic roar of the car's passage through the hundred-yard tunnel. The tone changed as the car slowed, started upgrade, changed again as it moved ahead on the level. They had emerged now onto the causeway linking the islands. Quickly the car built up speed. In six minutes they would pass over the Boca Ciega cut, the deep-water tidal-flow channel spanned by a single-lane bridge. Grayle tensed, counting silently to himself.

3

When Weather Control at Kennedy alerted the satellite that the weather-patrol craft was airborne, estimating five minutes to contact, the object of the meteorologists' attention had grown to an estimated diameter of four miles. Its rotation was clearly visible now.

"About five minutes for a complete revolution," Bunny said. "That means winds topping sixty at the periphery already. And she's holding position as if she'd dropped anchor."

"Kennedy is patching us directly in on the ground-to-air," Fred said. He plugged a hand microphone into a jack beside the screen. A faint crackle sounded; then the voice of the pilot came through loud and clear: *". . . getting dark fast, but it's clear as a bell out here, sea calm. I see some fishing boats down there, like ducks on a pond. I'm holding ten thousand . . ."*

"He ought to be spotting some sign of it," Bunny muttered. "He's within fifty miles of it—"

"Hold everything, Kennedy Tower." The pilot's tone changed. *"I have something . . . like a twister, a funnel. Black as soot. Looks kind of strange, hard edges like cast metal. Just sitting there on the horizon, maybe forty miles dead ahead."*

"Roger, Navy oh-nine-three," the Kennedy controller said. *"Close to ten miles and orbit the fix. Better give us the cameras on this from now on."*

"Cameras already rolling. I'm getting a hard echo off this thing. It's big, all right. It tops out at about fifteen thousand, six miles wide. It looks like a mountain standing on its nose. What's holding it up?"

"I've got him on the HR screen, sir," a junior technician called. "He's at thirty miles, closing fast."

"Say, Kennedy, I'm getting some turbulence now," the

Neptune pilot said calmly. "I'm making a pass east of the bogie. This thing is big. I never saw anything like this. It's opaque. It looks like it's spinning. Trailing streamers. The sea looks kind of funny under it. Black shadow, and . . ." There was a five-second pause. "There's a hole down there. A whirlpool. My God, I . . ."

"Navy oh-nine-three," Kennedy came in as the voice hesitated. "Repeat that last transmission."

"I'm down to five thousand, fifteen miles out. The thing's standing up over me like an umbrella. I'm holding about a twenty-degree crab. Winds are getting rough. I can hear it now, roaring . . ."

"All right, sheer off, Ken, get out of that turbulence—"

"There's a boat down there, some kind of boat! She's got her lights on. Looks like about a thirty-footer. She's got her stern to the twister. She's . . . my God, the damned thing's got her! She's going in!"

"Ken, get out of there!"

"There's three people aboard, I can see them!" the pilot was shouting now.

"All right, Navy oh-nine-three," another voice spoke harshly. "Report course change, and put some snap into it!"

"I'm . . . I'm making my pass now, north of it, five miles from contact. That boat—"

"Never mind the boat! Pick up a heading of oh-nine-oh and put some distance between you and this thing!"

"Turbulence is bad. She's fighting me . . ."

"Go to full gate, Ken! Get the hell out of there!"

"She's not reacting to control, Kennedy! She's . . . God! I'm getting knocked around . . . it'll tear her apart! . . ."

"Mr. Hoffa!" the technician called. "The Navy plane's headed right into it!"

"Ken! Try riding with it! Don't fight it, let it take you around, build up airspeed, and try to edge out!"

"Roger, Kennedy," the pilot said. His voice was flat,

emotionless now, against a background howl. "Tell the next guy to stay way back, twenty miles at least. It's like a magnet. I'm riding it like a merry-go-round. It's like a black well, two miles off my starboard wingtip. The noise— I guess you can hear it. I'm indicating four-fifty, but I'd say my ground speed is a couple hundred over that—"

"Ken, try a left turn, about five degrees—"

"I'm in a tight crab, no joy, Kennedy. The boat's coming under me again. It's right on the edge of the drop. It—it's breaking up. Ripped wide open. It's gone. Lucky at that. Fast. I'm getting the turbulence again. It's dark in here. I've got my nav lights on. It looks like black glass. Buffeting's bad now; can't take much of this . . . she . . ."

"Ken! Ken! Come in, Ken!"

"It merged," the technician said in a choked voice. "The plane flew right into it!"

4

The sound of the tires of the armored vehicle changed tone as it started across the metal-grid surface of the lift span of the Boca Ciega bridge. As they did, Grayle arched his back, putting pressure against the steel bar across his chest. For an instant it held firm; then it yielded, bent like sun-warmed wax. One end sprang free of the latch mechanism. At the sound, both guards tensed, their heads jerking around in time to see Grayle come to his feet, tense his forearms, and bend the chrome-steel rod between his wrists into a U, grip it with both hands, and with a quick twist snap it apart. The one called Randy made a strangled sound and clawed at the gun at his hip. Grayle plucked it from him, did something to it with his hands, threw it aside, in the same motion caught Jimbo as he rose, tapped him lightly against the wall, dropped him. He stepped to the rear of the car, gripped the steel rods which engaged slots at the sides of the double door, braced his feet, and lifted. One rod popped from its socket; the other broke with a crystalline tinkle. Grayle kicked the doors wide; a swirl of rain whipped at him. Gripping the jamb, he swung out, caught at the lamp housing above, pulled himself up onto the roof of the speeding vehicle. As he drew his legs up, there was a sharp double report, and a sharp pang stung his left shin.

He rose to his knees, looking down at the concrete railing flashing past, at the multistrand barbed wire above it, the dark water frothing whitecapped below. He rose to his feet against the rushing wind, gauged his distance, and dived far out over the pavement and the wires as the car braked, tires squealing, its siren bursting into howling life.

The escort spent half an hour patrolling the bridge on foot, playing powerful handlights across the water, but they found no sign of the escaped convict.

Under the high-beamed roof of the timbered farmhouse at Björnholm, the man who had been Gralgrathor sits at a long table, musing over a bowl of stout ale. In the fire burning on the hearth, images of faces and figures form, beckon, flicker away, their whispering flame-voices murmuring words in a tongue he has half-forgotten. Across the room Gudred sits on a bench between the two household servant girls, her youthful head bent over her needlework.

He pushes the bowl away, stands, belts a warm coat of bearskin about him. Gudred comes to him, the firelight soft on her plaited hair, the color of hammered gold.

"Will you sit with me by the fire awhile, my Grall?" she asked softly. Of all the daughters of Earl Arnulf, she alone had a voice that was not like the bawling of a bull calf. Her touch was gentle, her skin smooth and fair.

"You are a fool, Grall," the earl had said. "She is a sickly creature who will doubtless die bearing your first son. But if you indeed choose her over one of my lusty, broad-beamed wenches—why, take her, and be done with it!"

"I'm restless, girl," he tells her, smiling down into her face. "My head is fuddled with ale and too long lazing indoors. I need to walk the hills awhile to clear the cobwebs from my brain."

Her hand tightens on his arm. "Thor—not in the hills!

53

Not in the gloaming; I know you laugh at talk of trolls and ogres, but why tempt them—"

He laughs and hugs her close. Across the wide room, the curtains of the sleeping alcove stir. The face of a small boy appears, knuckling his eyes.

"See—we've waked Loki with our chatter," Gralgrathor says. "Sing him a song, Gudred, and by the time you've stitched another seam in your Fairday gown, I'll be back."

Outside, the light of the long northern evening gleams across the grain field which slopes down to the sea edge. Above, the forest mounts the steep rocks toward the pink-stained snowfields on the high ridges. With the old hound Odinstooth beside him, he sets off with long strides that in a quarter of an hour have put the home acre far below him.

Beside him, Odinstooth growls; he quiets the dog with a word. On the hillside, a movement catches his eye. It is a man, wrapped in a dark cloak, approaching from the tongue of the forest that extends down toward the farm. Grall watches him, noting his slim, powerful physique, his quick, sure movements.

The man's course leads him down across the fold of the earth, up again toward the ledge where Gralgrathor waits; there is something in his gait, his easy movements, that remind him of someone from the forgotten life. . . .

The man comes up the slope, his face shadowed under the cowl. For an instant, the heavy gray cloth looks like a Fleet-issue weather cloak. . . .

"Thor?" a mellow tenor voice calls.

Gralgrathor stands staring down at the newcomer, who has thrown back his cowl to reveal a lean, dark-eyed face, flame-red hair.

"Lokrien—am I dreaming?" Gralgrathor whispers.

The dark-eyed man smiles, shaking his head. He speaks

in a strange language . . . but dimly, Gralgrathor senses the meaning.

"Thor—man, it is you! Don't tell me you've forgotten your mother tongue!"

"After all these years?" Gralgrathor says. "You've really come?"

"I've come for you," Lokrien says in the half-strange language. "I've come to take you home, Thor."

Chapter Four

1

The governor of Caine Island prison stared incredulously at the chief of his guard force.

"You wouldn't be making some sort of ... of ill-considered joke, I suppose, Brasher?"

"No, sir," the wiry, dapper officer said. He stood at parade rest, looking acutely uncomfortable. Outside, the wind shrieked jeeringly.

"It's not possible," the governor said. "It simply *isn't possible!*"

"It happened on the bridge," the captain said, tight-mouthed. "Just as the car crossed the draw span."

"An escape." Hardman sat rigid in his chair, his face pale except for spots of color high on his cheeks. "From the country's only one-hundred-percent escape-proof confinement facility!"

The captain slanted his eyes at his superior.

"Governor, if you're suggesting ..."

"I'm suggesting nothing—except that a disaster has occurred!"

"He didn't get far," the captain said. "Not with two tranks in him. He went over the side into a riptide. That's a rough drop at sixty miles an hour, even without the storm. We're looking for the body, but—"

"I want the body found before the wires get the story! And if he's alive—" He stared fiercely at the officer.

"He's dead, sir, you can count on that—"

56

"If he's alive, I said, I want him caught, understand, Brasher? Before he reaches the mainland! Clear?"

The captain drew a breath and let it out, making a show of self-control.

"Yes, sir," he said heavily. "Just as you say." He turned away, giving Hardman a look as though there were comments only protocol prevented him from making.

When the officer had gone, Hardman sat for five minutes biting his thumb. Then he flipped the intercom lever.

"Lester, I want the Grayle dossier, everything we've got."

"There isn't much, Governor. You'll recall he was a transfer from Leavenworth East—"

"I want to see what we have."

Lester hesitated. "Is it true, Governor? The story going around is that he more or less burst his way through the side of an armored car—"

"That's an exaggeration! Don't help spread these damned rumors, Lester!"

"Of course, I knew it was ridiculous. I suppose under cover of the storm he caught the escort off guard—"

"I want those records right away, Lester. And get in touch with Pyle at Leavenworth, see if you can turn up anything else on Grayle. Check with Washington, the military services, the various federal agencies. Query Interpol and the UN PC Bureau. I want anything and everything you can turn up."

Lester whistled. "Quite a stir for just one man, sir, isn't it? I mean—"

"That man has my reputation in his pocket, Lester! I want to know all there is to know about him—just in case he *isn't* picked up washing around in the tide tomorrow morning!"

"Of course. You know, Governor, some of the staff have been repeating the stories about Grayle having served his time but not being released because the records were lost. They say he finally took the law into his own hands—"

"Nonsense. He'd have been free in ninety days."

"Just how long *had* he been on the inside sir? I was asking Captain Brasher, and he—"

"Get me the records, Lester," the governor cut him off. "I suggest you stop listening to rumors and get busy digging up some facts."

2

Lying flat among reeds on a shore of sulfurous black mud, Grayle averted his face from the howling wind that drove rain at him in icy sheets. He rested for a while, waiting for the dizziness to pass, then wormed his way up the bank, squinting against the downpour. A large tree afforded some slight shelter. He settled himself with his back to it, set about tearing strips from his prison garment to bind around his shin, in which a high-velocity pellet had scored a deep gouge before ricocheting off the bone.

On the highway above, a car churned past, a red strobe light flashing atop it, its headlights drowning in the almost solid downpour. Grayle set off along the shore, keeping in the shelter of scrub liveoak and Australian pines, slipping and sliding in the dark over the twisted roots. He was almost on the house before he saw it: a black cuboid of unpainted concrete, tin-roofed, dark and silent under the sodden trees. A small car stood in the sandy drive. Grayle went forward, skirted the vehicle. As he rounded it, a light lanced out from near the house, caught him full in the face.

"Its not worth stealing," a voice called over the drum of the rain. "But you're welcome to try."

The voice was that of a woman. Grayle stood where he was, waiting.

"You'd better be on your way," the voice said. "I keep a gun, you know. I have to, living where I do." She broke off; the light wavered.

"That's a prison jacket . . ."

The light moved over him, held on his face.

"You escaped from Caine Island?" When Grayle said nothing, she went on: "You better get inside, I heard the sirens a few minutes ago. They're patrolling the road."

Grayle took two swift steps, swept the light from her hand, reversed it, and flicked its beam across the woman. She was young, clean-featured, dark-haired, tall and slender, in a weatherproof trench coat. She didn't move, but turned her eyes aside from the light. There was no gun in her hands.

"I'm sorry," Grayle said. "I had to be sure." He handed the light back to her. Silently she turned, led the way into the house. She switched on a light, pulled down the roller shades. After the cold wind, the warmth and comparative silence enveloped Grayle like a downy blanket.

"You're hurt!" the girl said. Grayle braced his feet, fighting against a wave of dizziness.

"Lethanol!" The girl's voice came from a remote distance. "I can smell it on you! Sit down. . . ."

The girl stood over him, a concerned look on her face. Water dripped from her hair, running down her cheek. For an instant she reminded him of someone: the image of a face with ringleted hair and a mobcap flickered and was gone. He couldn't remember her name. It had been so long, there were so many things forgotten. . . .

He pushed himself to his feet; he must not sleep now.

She took his arm; he was aware of her voice but made no effort to follow the words. Fragments of old memories danced through his consciousness: a night in the rain on the field near Córdoba; standing by a stone wall, while booted feet tramped endlessly past, the blue-coated troops with their backpacks and fixed bayonets; a sudden, vivid evocation of the odor of tarred cordage and creaking timbers, of blown spume and salt fish, of leather and gunpowder. . . .

". . . stay on your feet," the girl was saying. "I saw a demonstration back at Bloomington . . ." Her voice was low, well modulated, her diction good.

He halted. "Do you have any high-protein food—meat, eggs? . . ."

"Yes. Good idea."

Grayle continued to pace up and down the small room. It was neat, clean, sparsely furnished with cheap plastic-and-steel-tube chairs and studio couch, a thin rug, a book-case built of bricks and boards and filled with paperbacks. Framed magazine pictures decorated the walls. There were flowers in foil-covered tin cans. The kitchen was an alcove with a fold-out table, a minimal counter-top refrigerator, a tiny electric range. The aroma of bacon and eggs was almost painfully sharp.

She put a plate on the table, added a big clay cup of black coffee.

"Eat slowly," she said, watching him swallow the egg in two bites. "It won't help you to get indigestion."

"How far am I from the perimeter wall?"

"About three miles as the crow flies, across the bay. Nearly seven by road. How did you get this far?"

"I swam."

"Yes, but . . ." Her eyes went to the crude bandage on his shin, visible under his pants cuff.

"You're hurt . . ." Without waiting for a reply, she knelt, with deft fingers opened the crude knot and pulled away the wet cloth. There was a faint pink scar across the tanned skin. She gave him a puzzled look as she rose.

"I'll move on now." He got to his feet. "I'm grateful to you for your kindness.

"What do you intend to do? Just walk out there and wait to be caught?"

"It will be better for you if you know nothing of my plans."

"You're on a peninsula here, there's only one way out. They'll have it blocked."

A car passed on the road. They listened as the growl of the engine receded.

"They'll be checking here soon," the girl said. "There's a crawl space above the kitchen."

"Why?"

"Why not?" Her tone was defiant.

"Why are you willing to involve yourself?"

"Perhaps I have a feeling for a man on the run."

He waited.

"I had a brother at Caine Island. That's why I bought this place—I was allowed to see him one day a week. He had nobody else; and neither did I."

"That doesn't explain—"

"He's dead. Three months ago. Leukemia, they said. He was only thirty-four."

"You blame the authorities?"

"They had him," she said flatly.

Scarlet light struck the front window, glowed through the gap under the blind. A brilliant white light replaced it, pushing shadows across the floor. The growl of an engine was audible over the rattle of rain on the roof.

"We waited too long," the girl said tightly.

"Stay out of the way, out of sight," Grayle said. Outside, car doors slammed. He flattened himself against the wall beside the door. There was a sharp rap. A moment later the knob turned, the door was thrown violently open. Rain blasted in. There was the sound of metal rasping on leather, the click of a safety catch being snapped off. A tall man in a shiny yellow slicker took a step into the room. Grayle moved then, caught the man's gun hand, jerked him to him.

"Don't cry out," he said into the cop's startled face.

"Harmon!" the man yelled. "Don't—"

Grayle gripped him by the shoulder, gave him a sharp shake. He went slack. Grayle lowered him to the floor. The second man came through the door at a dead run. As he passed Grayle rapped him on the side of the neck; he fell hard, lay still. Grayle pushed the door shut. The girl's eyes met his.

"I never saw anyone move so quickly—"

"Good-bye," Grayle cut her off, "and thank you—"

"What are you going to do?"

"Don't involve yourself, Miss—"

"Rogers. Anne Rogers." She avoided looking at the two unconscious men on the floor. "And I'm already involved."

"I'll be all right, Miss Rogers."

"Take my car."

"I never learned to drive one."

Her eyes searched his face. "Then I'll have to go with you."

She flicked off the lights, took out her flash, opened the door, stepped out into the rain. Grayle followed. She reached inside the police car, switched off the lights. The radio crackled and muttered.

The inside of the small car smelled wet and moldy. The starter groaned sluggishly.

"I'll have to try to jump it from their car." Anne got out and went back to the trunk, opened it, took out a pair of heavy insulated cables. Grayle lifted the hood for her as directed, watched as she attached the big copper alligator clips, making sparks jump and sputter.

This time the starter whirled energetically; the engine coughed, broke into stuttering life. She revved it, sending clouds of exhaust rolling past the window.

"Hold your foot on the gas," she said, and jumped out of the car to disconnect the cables. The deck lid thumped. She slid back in beside him.

"Here we go. Be thinking about how to handle it when we get to the causeway."

For ten minutes they drove through torrential rain, doing a reckless twenty miles per hour on the glossy blacktop. Gusts of wind threw the light car across the road. No other cars passed them. At one point, water was across the road; Anne shifted down and crawled through. Then lights shone a hundred yards ahead. The red beacon of a parked police car blinked through the rain.

"Stop the car."

She braked, pulled over, looked at him inquiringly.

"Can you face it out if they search the car?" he asked.

"What are you going to do?"

"I'll ride the frame."

"You can't. There's nothing to ride on, no room—"

"I'll manage." He stepped out into the storm, went flat, and eased under the chassis. He felt over the rust-pitted frame, scalded his fingers on the exhaust stack, groped for a handhold on a cross member. He hooked the toes of his prison-issue shoes over the rear spring hangars, lifted his body from the wet pavement, pressing against the underside of the car. The girl crouched by the car, staring at him.

"You *are* crazy! You can't hold on that way! If you slip—you'll be killed!"

"Go ahead, Anne," he said. "I'm all right."

She hesitated for a moment; then she nodded and was gone. Grayle heard the gears shift; the car lurched as it started ahead. Acrid gases leaked from the rotted pipes; the car vibrated, jolting over the road. Oily water sleeted at him; gravel stung him. The tires hissed, close to his face. Then the car slowed. Lights shone on the pavement, gliding nearer. He saw the wheels of another car; two pairs of booted feet approached, stopped a foot from his head. Voices, indistinct over the rumble of the steady rain and the whine of the wind. Doors clanked; the car swayed, and the girl's feet appeared. One policeman rounded the car; more door slams, more rocking. The deck lid opened and slammed. The girl got back into the driver's seat. The masculine boots withdrew. The car pulled ahead, accelerated.

Half a mile farther on, it slowed to a halt. Grayle dropped clear and crawled out into the downpour. He slid into the seat and met the girl's eyes.

"I still don't believe it," she said. "No one could do what you just did."

Grayle put his hand on the door.

"Thanks," he said. "I'll leave you now."

"What's your name?" the girl asked suddenly.

"Grayle."

"Why were you . . . there?" She tilted her head toward the invisible island behind them.

"I killed a man." He watched her eyes.

"In a fair fight?"

"He almost killed me, if that's what you mean."

"Grayle, you wouldn't last a day without me. You've been inside too long."

"I have a long way to go, Anne."

"Doesn't everyone, Grayle?"

He hesitated for a moment; then he nodded.

She smiled tensely, pulled the car back onto the road, and gunned ahead along the dark road.

They sit in the big, drafty hall, hung with shields and spears and axes which are not decorations but are ready to use, beside the great granite fireplace, chimneyless and smoky.

"It's a strange, barbaric world you found yourself castaway on, Thor," Lokrien says. "But you've a roof over your head, a warm fire on a cold night, good food and ale, a woman to comfort you. It could have been worse."

"I found friends here," Gralgrathor says. "They could have killed me, but instead they let me into their lives."

"Poor creatures. I wonder what their history is? They're human, of course, no doubt descendants of some ancient spacefarers wrecked here long ago. Have they any legends of their lost homeland?"

Gralgrathor nods. "It must have been long ago. Their myths are much distorted."

"There's a certain peace and simplicity here—the peace of ignorance," Lokrien says. "They've never heard of the Xorc. They don't dream that out there a great Imperial Fleet is defending their little world against an enemy that could vaporize the planet. Perhaps in years to come, Thor, you'll look back sometimes with nostalgia on your idyll among the primitives."

"No, Loki," Gralgrathor says. "It's not earth I'll look

back on with nostalgia. I'm staying here, Loki. I'm not going back with you."

Lokrien shakes his head as if to clear it of some dark vision. "You don't know what you're saying. Never to go back? Never to see Ysar, to wear the uniform again, to sail with the Fleet—"

"All those things, Loki."

"Do you know what I did to come here?" Lokrien says. "I deserted my post in the line of battle. I waited for a lull and turned my boat and drove for this outpost world to look for you. It took me all these years of searching to pick up the trace from your body shield circuitry and find you here. With luck we can concoct a story to explain how I found you—"

"Loki, I can't desert my home, my wife, my child."

"You'd let this savage female and her cub stand in the way of ..." Lokrien hesitated. "I'm sorry, Thor. The woman is beautiful. But Ysar! You'd give up your whole life for this barn, these grubby fields, this petty barony—"

"Yes."

"Then think of your duty to the Fleet."

"The Fleet is only a collection of machines, once the dream behind it is gone."

"You think you'll find the dream, as you call it, here on this backwoods world?"

"Better a live acorn than a dead forest, Loki."

Loki looks across the gulf at the brother he had come to find. "I could force you, Thor. I still have my suit and my Y-gun."

Gralgrathor smiles a little.

"Don't try to decide now," Lokrien says. "We're both tired. We need sleep. In the morning—"

"In the morning nothing will have changed."

"No? Perhaps you're wrong about that."

"There are clean furs there, on the hearth," Gralgrathor says. "Sleep well, Loki. I need to walk for a while."

Lokrien's eyes follow Gralgrathor as he steps out into the icy moonlight.

Chapter Five

1

"Let me get this straight," the commander of the Lake-wood Naval Air Station said grimly. "You're telling me I lost a pilot in broad daylight, in a *whirlpool?*"

"Not precisely that, Commodore Keyes," the colonel said. "There's a tremendous volume of air involved in this thing, too. Friction with the water surface, you understand—"

"No, I don't understand. Maybe you'd better start at the beginning."

"I have the recording of the pilot's transmissions here, in the event you'd care to hear it."

The commodore nodded curtly. The colonel hastily set up the small portable player, adjusted the tape. In a moment the pilot's voice was coming through crisply.

The two men listened in silence, following the recon plane's progress. The commodore's face was set in a scowl as the tape ended.

"All right, what are we doing about this thing?"

"The nucleus of the disturbance is centered on a point northwest of Bermuda." The colonel stepped to the large world map on the wall and indicated the spot. "It's growing steadily larger, setting up powerful winds and currents over an area of several thousand square miles. Water is being pulled in toward the center from every direction, thus the whirlpool." The colonel produced a stack of photos from his briefcase and passed them across the desk. They showed a great, glossy-black funnel, wrapped in dusty spirals like disintegrating cotton-wool batting.

"Those were made with ultraviolet from about a hundred miles out. You'll note the calibration marks; they show that the throat of the whirlpool is approximately a tenth of a mile wide at the surface—"

"How wide?"

"I know it sounds incredible, Commodore, but I have it on good assurance that the figure of five hundred feet is accurate."

"Hopper, do you have any idea of the volume of water you're talking about?"

"Well, I could work it out—"

"How deep is the sea at this point?"

"I don't have the exact figure, sir, but it *is* deep ocean there, well off the continental shelf—"

"What kind of force would it take to get that much water moving at the velocity this thing must have? Where's the energy coming from?"

"Well, Commodore—"

"And you say water is flowing *in* from every direction. Where's it going? And the air: thousands of cubic miles of air on the move, all toward the same point. What's happening to it? Where's the outflow?"

"Commodore, we have aircraft out now photographing the entire eastern half of the country, and well out into the Atlantic. And of course the satellite is busy on this thing as well. I hope to have some results very soon now."

"Find out where that water's going, Hopper. There's something wrong here. We're missing something. That water has to be somewhere. I want to know where, before the biggest tidal wave in history hits the east coast!"

2

In the governor's office at Caine Island, Lester Pale, special aide to the governor, shook his head ruefully at his chief.

"The Grayle dossier isn't much, I'm afraid, sir," he said. "I have the documents covering his transfer from Leavenworth East six years ago; they're in order. And of course his record here at Caine Island. But prior to that . . ." Lester shook his head.

"Give me what you've got." Hardman spoke impatiently. He was hunched forward over the desk, raising his voice above the drumming of the rain that had increased steadily now for nearly six hours.

"I talked to Warden Pyle as you suggested, sir. Many of his records were lost in a file-room fire about twelve years ago; but he says that of his own memory he recalls that Grayle was a military prisoner, in for the murder of an army officer."

"Go on."

"The funny thing is, Governor, he was absolutely certain that Grayle was an inmate when he took over East L, nearly twenty years ago." He paused, looking dubiously at his superior.

"So?"

"Well, after all, sir—how old *is* Grayle?"

"You tell me."

"Well, sir—Pyle called in an old con, a man who had done twenty years of a life sentence before parole. He works in the prison kitchens now. Pyle asked him what he remembered about Grayle."

"And?"

Lester made a disclaiming gesture. "The old fellow said that Grayle was one of the prisoners transferred from

Kansas along with him, back in seventy-one. And that he had known him before that."

"How long before that?"

"For over ten years. In fact, he swears Grayle was an inmate when he started his stretch. And that, Governor, was almost thirty-five years ago. So you see what I'm talking about."

"What *are* you talking about, Lester? Spell it out."

"Why, they're obviously confusing the man with someone else. There may have been another prisoner with the name Grayle, possibly someone with a physical resemblance. I don't suppose they've had occasion to think of the man for a number of years, and now they're dredging up false memories, superimposing our Grayle on what they recall of the older man."

"What about the army records of the court-martial?"

Lester shook his head. "No success there so far, sir. I have a friend in the Pentagon who has access to a great deal of retired material that's never been programmed into the Record Center. He supplies data to historians and the like; they get a lot of requests. Just for the sake of thoroughness I asked him to dig back as far as he can. But he informed me just a few minutes ago that he went back as far as World War Two and turned up nothing."

"Did you tell him to keep looking?"

"Well, no, sir. That's already thirty-six years back. He's hardly likely—"

"Tell him to keep digging, Lester. You don't send a man to prison for life without making a record of it somewhere."

"Governor," a voice spoke sharply on the intercom. "Captain Brasher to see you. He insisted I break in—"

"Send him in."

The door opened and the guard chief strode into the room, gave Pale a sharp look, stood waiting.

"Well, speak up, man!" the governor snapped.

."As I suspected, sir," the captain said, "Grayle's alive. He overpowered one of my officers and a state patrolman in a shack on the north shore, beat them into unconsciousness, and got clear."

"Got clear? Aren't the roads blocked?"

"Certainly. I don't mean he's escaped the net, just that he's still at large."

"How long ago was this?"

The captain's eyes snapped to the wall clock, snapped back. "Just under half an hour."

"Was the shack occupied?"

"Ah—I can't say as to that—"

"Find out. How did he leave? In the patrol car?"

"No, it was parked in front of the place. That's how—"

"Find out what kind of car the occupant owned. Meanwhile, watch every road. He can't be far away. And, Brasher—don't let him slip through your fingers. I don't care what you have to do to stop him—stop him!"

"I'll stop him, all right." Brasher hesitated. "You know he's attacked three of my men now—"

"That doesn't say a hell of a lot for your men, Brasher. Tell them to get on their toes and stay there!"

"That's what I wanted to hear you say, Governor." Brasher wheeled and left the room.

"Governor," Lester said, "I have a feeling that somewhere along the line there's been a serious mistake—"

"Don't talk like a fool, Lester. Grayle's commitment papers are in order; I have that much—"

"I don't mean an error on your part, Governor. I mean prior to his transfer to Caine Island. Possibly that's why he made this rather desperate break. Perhaps he's innocent—"

Hardman leaned forward, his big hands flat on the desk.

"He broke out of a prison under my command, Lester. I have twenty-one years invested in this business without an escape, and I'm not letting anyone blot a perfect record, clear?"

"Governor, this is a man's life—"

"And of course there's more to it than just my reputation," Hardman said, leaning back. "If one man crashed out of Caine—and got clear—we'd have every malcontent on the inside making a try. It would be a blow at the entire modern penological system—"

"Brasher will shoot him down like a dog, Governor!"

"I gave no such orders."

"Brasher will interpret them that way!"

"He can interpret them any way he likes, Lester—as long as he nails his man, I won't be overly critical of his methods!"

3

"I'm not interested in excuses, Mr. Hunnicut," the voice of the Deputy Undersecretary of the Interior for Public Power rasped in the ear of the chief engineer at Pasmaquoddie. "I've gone out on a limb for you people; now I expect answers from you that I can give to the Committee. They're looking for scalps, and they think mine will do!"

"I've already explained that there seems to be a transmission loss greatly in excess of the theoretical factor, Mr. Secretary—"

"Meaning the system is a failure! Don't fall back on the kind of jargon you technical people use to obfuscate the issues when things go wrong! I want it in plain language! Your generating station is drawing ten percent over its rated operational standard, while the receiving stations report anywhere from thirty- to forty-percent effectiveness. Now, just tell me in words of one syllable—where is all that power going, Mr. Hunnicut?"

"It's obvious there's a leakage somewhere, Mr. Secretary," Hunnicut said, holding his temper with an effort.

"Where? In the transmission end? In the receiving stations? Or in the giant brains that dreamed up this fiasco?"

"Mr. Secretary, this is a wholly new area of technology! There are bound to be certain trial-and-error adjustments—"

"Hogwash! You didn't mention that when you were pleading with Appropriations for another hundred million!"

"Look here, this isn't as simple a matter as tracing the point of breakdown in a conventional line-transmission system—and even there, it sometimes takes days to pinpoint the trouble. Remember the New York blackout in the sixties, and—"

"Don't give me a history lesson, Hunnicut! Are you telling me that anybody and his dog Rex can tap our broadcast system at will, and there's nothing we can do about it?"

"Wait a minute, I didn't say that—"

"The newspapers will say it! Give me a better line to feed to them!"

"Mr. Secretary, you have to understand, we have no instruments, no procedures for this situation! It's totally unprecedented, contrary to theory, inexplicable—"

"It's happening, Mr. Hunnicut! Better realign your theories!"

"We've made a start. We've rigged some makeshift field-density sensors, and I have four motorized teams out running retiring search curves, plotting the gradient—"

"Meaning what?"

"Meaning that with luck we'll detect a pattern that will enable us to triangulate on the point of power drain."

"Back to that! I can't give that to the press, Hunnicut! They'll drag in everything from Russians to Little Green

Men from Mars! 'Aliens steal U.S. power' I can see the headlines now!"

"It's nothing like that! I'm pretty sure we'll find it's some sort of anomalous natural formation that's drawing off the energy! A massive ore deposit, something of that sort!"

"Hunnicut—you're babbling! Just between us—what do you really think it is that's drinking a couple of hundred thousand killowatts per hour out of the air?"

"Mr. Secretary, I don't know."

"I'm glad you admit it, Hunnicut. Now, I suggest you get busy and find out, before I yank you out of that plush office and put in somebody with a little better grasp of the dynamics of modern politico-technology!"

"I'm no politician! I—"

"Locate that leak, Hunnicut—or you'll be back taking gamma counts on the Lackawanna pile!"

4

Anne Rogers stared out through the rain-blurred wind-shield at the almost invisible road surface unwinding ahead. At wide intervals the lights of a lonely house shone weakly through the downpour slanting through the head-lights.

"There's a town about five miles ahead," she said. "We should change cars there."

They rode in silence for a few minutes. More lights appeared ahead. They passed a gas station, dark and deserted. Anne made a left turn at a blinking yellow traffic light, followed a broad truck route for half a mile, then took a right into a narrow residential street. The trees lining the way provided some shelter from the rain. They moved along at a crawl, lights dimmed. There were cars parked at the side of the curbless street and in the weed-grown yards.

"They're worse wrecks than this one," Anne said, accelerating past an empty stretch. "We might as well pick a good one while we're at it."

"I'll rely on your judgment," Grayle said with a hint of humor.

Anne glanced at him sideways. "You were inside so long, I suppose everything looks strange to you. My God, what a terrible thing, to take a man's freedom away! I'd rather be killed and be done with it."

"It wasn't as bad as all that. There's a certain peace to be found in the monastic life, after . . ."

"After what?" she asked softly.

He shook his head. "You wouldn't understand, I'm afraid, Anne. You're so young. So terribly young—"

"I'm twenty-five, Grayle. You're not more than thirty-five?"

He didn't answer. They passed through a green light, went along a deserted block of elderly storefronts, a few of which had suffered incongruous face-lifts which accentuated the shabbiness of the neighborhood. They slowed at a vacant lot where a row of identical stamped-steel grilles and flimsy bumpers fronted a cracked sidewalk under a string of draggled pennants which beat in the wind like trapped birds. A faded sign read: HERB GRINER FORD.

"New cars," Anne said. "But we'd need the keys."

"Explain, please."

"You need the ignition key to start a car with. And even to get the doors open. They probably keep them locked in the office."

"Drive around the corner and stop there in the shadows."

She swung around the corner and pulled into the black pool under a giant live oak.

"Wait here." Grayle stepped from the car, crossed the street briskly, threaded his way between the cars to the back door of the small shed. He gripped the knob, gave it a quick twist; metal tinkled. He stepped inside and closed the door.

There was a small desk, a plastic-upholstered chair with a burst seam, a calendar on the wall. Wan light from a pole-mounted lamp at the curb shone on a filing cabinet, a scrap of worn rug, a clothes tree with a battered hat.

Grayle tried the center drawer of the desk; it popped open with a small splintering sound. There were papers, rubber bands, paper clips, loose cigarettes, some pennies, a pocketknife. He tried the other drawers. The bottom one on the right contained a garishly colored cigar box with a curled lid. Inside were bunches of keys, four to a ring, each with an attached tag. Grayle scanned them: White 2 Dr Fal; Gray 4 Dr Gal . . .

The door beside Grayle made a faint sound. He turned as it flew suddenly open. A man stepped in, holding a heavy revolver in front of him. He was bald, middle-aged, bulky in a tan hunting jacket, water-soaked across the shoulders, the collar turned up. He wore round-lensed steel glasses, water-misted. A drop of water hung from the tip of his prominent nose.

"All right, just turn around and put your hands up again' the wall, boy," he said in a high-pitched, nasal drawl. He took a step sideways and reached for the telephone on the desk. Grayle hadn't moved. The man paused, his hand on the phone.

"By God, I told you to move!"

"Didn't Herb tell you about me?" Grayle asked casually.

"Hah?" The man stared. "What the hell you mean?"

"The idea was that I'd drop by to amfrunct the baterpomp, the grillik frens. Just until the rain lets up, you understand."

"Oh." The man was frowning; the gun dropped. "By God, why didn't he let me know—"

There was a sound from the door; the man with the gun

whirled, bringing it up; Grayle took a step, struck him on the side of the neck with his right hand as his left swept over the weapon, snatched it clear. The man fell against the wall. Anne stood in the doorway, a lug wrench in her hand, her eyes wide.

"I told you to wait," Grayle said harshly.

"I . . . I saw him get out of one of the cars."

"Don't nursemaid me, girl." Grayle picked up the keys from the desk. "Can you decode these notations?"

She glanced at the tags and nodded. She looked at the man on the floor. He was breathing noisily.

"He's not hurt," Grayle said. "He'd have shot you," he added.

"You're a strange man, Grayle. You'd really care if he shot me, wouldn't you? And even him—and those two policemen: you knew what you were doing, didn't you? You know just where to hit them, and how hard, to knock them unconscious without really hurting them. That's important to you, isn't it—not to really hurt anybody?"

"We'd better go," Grayle said.

"I *was* nursemaiding you," Anne said. "I suppose the idea you couldn't drive, didn't know your way around, gave me the feeling you were helpless. But you're not helpless. You're less helpless than any man I ever saw."

"Which machine?" Grayle asked brusquely.

"The white Falcon," the girl said.

"What?" the word was explosively sharp.

She stared at him. "We'll take the white Falcon. They're very common."

They found the car in the front row; it started easily; the gauge showed half a tank. There was a stale odor of cigarette smoke in the car; a folded map lay on the seat.

"They've been using this one. That's good. It'll be broken in." Anne examined the map. "We'll cut across to nineteen on fifty and head north. With a little luck, we'll be across the state line before daylight."

At the top of the ridge known as Snorri's Ax, Odins-tooth whines, sniffing the air. Gralgrathor strokes the old hound's blunt head. The dog's growl ends in a sharp, frightened yap.

"It takes more than a bear to make you nervous, old warrior. What is it?" Gralgrathor stares downward through the night toward the faint spark far below that is the firelight shining from his house.

"Time we went back," he murmurs. "The moon's down; morning soon."

He is half a mile from the house when he hears the scream, faint and muffled, quickly shut off. In an instant he is running, the big dog bounding ahead.

The servants are clustered in the houseyard, holding torches high. Big, bowed-backed Hulf comes to meet him, a knobbed club gripped in his hands. Tears run down his sun-and-ice-burned face into the stained nest of his beard.

"You come too late, Grall," he says. The big dog halts, stands stiff-legged, hackles up, snarling. Gralgrathor pushes through the silent huddle of housecars. The bodies lie outside the threshold: Gudred, slim and golden-haired, the blood scarlet against her ice-white face. For an instant her dead eyes seem to meet his, as if to communicate a message from an infinite distance. The boy lies half under her, face down, with blood in his fair hair. Odinstooth *crouches flat at the sound that comes from his master's throat.*

"We heard the boy cry out, Grall," an old woman says. "We sprang from our nests and ran here, to see the troll scuttling away, there . . ." She points a bony finger up the rocky slope.

"Loki—where is he?"

"Gone." The old woman sags. "Changed into his black were-shape and fled—"

Gralgrathor plunges into the house. The embers on the hearth show him the empty room, shadow-crowded, the fallen hangings ripped from the sleeping alcove, the glossy spatter of blood across the earthen floor. Behind him, a man comes through the doorway, his torch making great shadows which leap and dance against the dark walls.

"Gone, Grall, as old Siv said. Not even a troll would linger after such handiwork as this."

Gralgrathor catches up a short-handled iron sledge hafted with oak. The men scatter as he bursts from the house.

"Loki," he screams, "where are you?" Then he is running, and the great hound leaps at his side.

Chapter Six

1

Aboard the weather satellite, the meteorologists on duty, as well as half the off-duty staff, were gathered in the main observation deck, watching the big screens which showed a view of the night side of the planet below. Faint smudges of diffuse light marked the positions of the great metropolitan areas along the eastern American seaboard. A rosy arc still embraced the western horizon, fading visibly with the turn of the planet. The voice of the observer on duty at Merritt Island came from the big wall annunciator, marred by static.

". . . the turbulence is on an unprecedented scale, which plays hell with observation, but we've run what we have through the computer. The picture that's building is a pretty strange one. We get a pattern of an expanding circular front, centered off Bermuda. The volumes of air involved are staggering. Winds have reached one hundred fifty knots now, at fifty miles from the center. We're getting a kind of rolling action: high air masses being drawn down, dumping ice crystals, then rolling under and joining in the main Coriolis rotation. The jetstream is being affected as far away as Iceland. All southern-route flights are being diverted north. Meanwhile, the temperature off the Irish coast is dropping like an express elevator. It looks very much as if the Gulf Stream is being pulled off course and dissipated down into the South Atlantic."

Fred Hoffa, senior meteorologist, exchanged puzzled looks with the satellite commander.

"We hear you, Tom," he said into his hand-held microphone. "But we don't quite understand this. What you're describing is a contradiction in terms. You have all that cold, high-altitude air rushing in: what's pulling it? Where's it going? Same for the ocean currents. We've been plotting the data, and it looks like a lot of water flowing toward the storm center, nothing coming out. It doesn't make much sense."

"I'm just passing on what the tapes tell me, Fred. I know it sounds screwy. And some of the data are probably faulty. But the pattern is plain enough. Wait until daylight, and you'll see it for yourself."

The general took the microphone. "Merritt Island, we've been studying this thing by IR, radar, and laser, and all we can make of it is one hell of a big whirlpool—just what that Neptune pilot described."

"It's not exactly a normal whirlpool. It's more like what you see when the water runs down a bathtub drain."

"Yes, but that's . . ." Fred's voice died away.

"Now you're getting the idea," Tom said. "We estimate that two-point-five cubic miles of seawater have poured down that hole in the last six hours."

"But—where's it going?"

"That's a good question. Let us know down here if you figure out an answer."

2

A taxi was parked at the curb before the narrow front of an all-night eatery. The driver was inside, hunched on a stool over a cup of coffee. He turned as the door opened, gave the big man who came in a hard-eyed look, turned back to the counterman.

"So I told him, I said, what the hell, nobody tells John

Zabisky how to drive. I says, look, Mac, I'm eighteen years in the hacking game, and I've drove all kinds, and I don't take nobody telling me—"

"Excuse the intrusion, Mr. Zabisky," the newcomer said. "I need a cab, urgently."

The cabbie turned slowly. "How you know my name?"

"You mentioned it just now."

"Who're you?"

"Falconer is the name. As I said, it's urgent—"

"Yeah, yeah, hold your water. Everything's urgent to you guys. To me this cup of java's urgent."

The counterman was leaning on one elbow, working on a molar with a broomstraw. He withdrew it and examined the tip, smiling sourly.

"Refill, John?"

"Hell yes, sure, why not?"

"It's worth fifty dollars to me to get to Princeton immediately," the man who called himself Falconer said.

"Princeton? New Jersey? In this weather? You nuts or something? I wouldn't drive it in daylight for fifty bucks."

"You're off duty?"

"Naw, I'm not off duty. Why?"

"Your license says you'll take a customer where he wants to go—for the fare on the meter."

"Get this guy," John said, staring at Falconer's smooth, unlined face. "What are you, kid, playing hooky? Your old lady know you're out at this time o' night?"

Falconer smiled gently. "Like to come outside with me, Zabisky?"

The husky driver came off the stool in a rush which somehow lost momentum as he crowded against Falconer; he found himself eased gently backward. It hadn't been like running into a brick wall—not exactly.

"Hey, not inside, John," the counterman spoke up. "But you can take him in the alley. I like to see these wise guys get it."

The cabby whirled on him. "How'd you like me to come around there and cave in a few slats for you, loudmouth? Whatta you trying to do, lose me a fare?" He jerked his mackinaw straight and gave Falconer a sideways look.

"I'll take twenty now," he said. "Where in Princeton you want to go?"

It was a long drive through rain that gusted and swirled across the car glass like a battery of fire hoses. On the outskirts of the town, the cabby mumbled, peering ahead, negotiating the twists and turns of the road down which Falconer had directed him. The headlights picked up a pair of massive wrought-iron gates set in a high brick wall.

"Dim your lights three times," Falconer instructed as the cab pulled up facing the gates. The gates swung back on a graveled drive. They went along it, halted before wide steps, a colonnaded veranda behind which tall windows reflected blackness and the shine of the headlights on wet leaves.

"Looks like nobody home," the driver said. "Who lives here?"

"I do." Rain swirled in Falconer's face as he opened the door on the left side. "We have some unfinished business, Mr. Zabisky," he said. He stepped out and turned; the driver's door flew open, and Zabisky bounded out, a tire iron in his knobbed fist.

"O.K., mister, start something," he bawled over the sounds of the storm. Falconer moved toward him; an instant later the tire iron was skidding across the drive. Empty-handed, Zabisky faced Falconer, an expression of astonishment on his wide face.

"That makes it more even, don't you think, Zabisky?" Falconer called. The driver put his head down and plowed in, both fists swinging. Falconer took a solid blow on the chest before he tied him up, spun him, held him with both arms locked behind his back.

"Ready to surrender, Zabisky?"

"Go to hell!" The cabbie tried to kick Falconer's shin. He gave his arms another twist of the cloth.

"Ask me nicely, and I'll let you go."

"Have your fun, mister," Zabisky grunted. "Break 'em off at the elbow. I ask you nothin'."

Falconer released the man; he turned at bay, fists cocked. His thick black hair was plastered across his wide, low forehead. He licked rain off his lips, waiting.

"Zabisky, do you have a family? Anyone who'll worry if you don't come home for a few days?"

"What's it to you?"

"I need a man who doesn't wilt under pressure. You'll do. I'll pay you a hundred dollars a day plus expenses."

"Shove it, mister."

"Two hundred."

"You nuts or something?"

"I'm offering you a job. I had to know something about you first. Don't feel badly about not being able to use that tire iron on me. I'm a professional fighter."

Zabisky frowned. "What you want me to do? I don't go for the rough stuff."

"I want you to drive my car."

"Two cees a day for a chauffeur?"

"It's my money." Falconer took out folded money, handed over two hundred-dollar bills. Zabisky looked at them.

"Where to?"

"Anywhere I tell you."

Zabisky considered. "This on the level?"

"Why would I waste your time and mine? Come inside and we'll talk about it." Falconer turned and went up the steps. After a moment Zabisky tucked the bills away and followed.

3

In the governor's office at Caine Island, Captain Brasher of the guard force stood before his chief's desk, looking uncomfortable.

"The house belongs to a Mrs. Talbot," he was saying. "A widow, age about twenty-five. Not bad-looking—"

"Never mind her looks. Where is she?"

"We haven't found her yet. But—"

"Any signs of violence in the house?"

"Not unless you want to include two men stretched on the floor," Brasher snapped.

"Did they see who attacked them?"

"They haven't been able to tell us anything useful. You know how these concussion cases are, Governor. Harmon says he didn't see who hit him. Weinert has no memory of anything since yesterday's ball game."

"What about the woman's car?"

"A fifty-nine Rambler, pale tan with white top, license number 40 D 657, dent in right-front fender."

"Has it been seen?"

"It went through the north causeway roadblock at twelve-thirteen. The woman was driving. She was alone."

"Are you sure of that?"

"The sheriff's boys went over the car with a fine-tooth comb, naturally. It was clean."

"Any other cars pass the roadblock?"

"Not a one. Most people know enough to stay home in this weather."

"What else do you know about the woman?"

"She's lived in the shack for the past couple of years. She had a brother who was an inmate here; he died last March. She used to visit him. I don't know why she hung around afterward—"

"Tell me more about the car. Was there anything unusual about it? Any bundles on the back seat, rug on the floor, anything at all?"

"My boys would have caught anything like that. The car was clean. At the time, we had no reason to hold the woman—"

"Where was she going at that hour, in this weather?"

"She was on her way to relatives in the northern part of the state; she was worried about flooding—"

"Where in the northern part of the state?"

"Gainesville, she said."

"Get the names of these relatives?"

"Well . . . no."

"Does she have any relatives in Gainesville?"

"Well—"

"Find out, Brasher. And put out a general alert on the car. I want it found fast. And when it's found, I want it gone over with magnifying glasses; over, in, and under!"

"Naturally I've alerted the State Highway Patrol," Brasher said. "But frankly, Governor, I don't understand all this emphasis on the car. The woman obviously left the house before Grayle arrived. He found the house empty and broke in—"

"Any signs of that?"

"Well, the locks weren't broken. But—" He broke off, looking astounded. "By God! It's clear as day! The little bitch was in on it! They planned it in advance! She was waiting for him, with the car gassed up and ready to go—"

"Planned it two and a half years in advance—including the death of the brother? And I thought you said she was alone in the car. But never mind. Check on the car. Find out where it was serviced, what kind of shape it was in, whether she had any special work done on it. Talk to her friends. Find out if she ever met Grayle, ever visited the prison after her husband died. And Captain . . ." He held Brasher's eyes with a cold expression. "I'll bet you my retirement to your next promotion you don't find a thing."

The guard chief returned the glare. "I'll take that bet—sir."

4

Chief Engineer Hunnicut, arriving seven minutes late for his scheduled briefing of the officials assembled in the office of the regional director, USPPA, looked around at the grim expressions lining the long table.

"I won't waste your time with generalities, gentlemen. You're aware that some difficulties have developed in the first hours of operation of the APU station. In essence, it boils down to a rather wide discrepancy between rated and actual efficiency. This in turn suggests a power leakage, which at first glance appears preposterous. A very specialized type of receiver is required to draw power from the transmission field—"

"It was our understanding that nothing of the sort was possible," a jowly man with a mane of gray hair cut in brusquely. "I recall the objections raised in the early hearings, and the contemptuous way in which those objections were put down by you so-called technical people. And you have the effrontery to stand up here and tell us power is leaking—or being stolen—from the U.S. government."

"I don't know who you've been talking to, Senator," Hunnicut said. "But *I* said nothing whatever about power being stolen. I think it would be wise to avoid leaping to any conclusions at this point—particularly before you've heard what I came here to report to you."

"Well, it certainly appears obvious . . ." The senator trailed off.

"It's far from obvious. This is a new technology, gentlemen. Even those of us who designed and constructed the system don't pretend to know all the answers; I think it would behoove others with less knowledge of the facts to exercise some restraint in the ideas they spread abroad; those comments may come home to roost." Hunnicut swept the table with a challenging look. "Now, as to what we've turned up—it appears that there are at least two field discontinuities, other than those accounted for by the nine receiving stations."

"What's a field discontinuity?"

"A point of demand on the power field creates a distinctive fluctuation in the field-strength gradient. We're dealing with what might be described as force lines, analogous to the force lines of a magnetic field. When power is drawn, these force lines are bent toward the point of demand."

"Well—where are these illegal receivers? What are you doing about them? Whom have you notified? Do you intend to allow them to simply continue to drain off God knows how many thousands of kilowatts of government-owned power, and thumb their noses at us?"

"The pinpointing of these discontinuities is not quite so simple as locating an illegal radio transmitter, for example. It's necessary to take a large number of field-strength readings, and to plot them against the theoretical flux-density pattern. Again I remind you that the state of the art—"

"We're not here to listen to a lecture on art," the senator cut in. "I've asked you a number of questions, young man, and I expect—"

"I'm no longer a young man, Senator," Hunnicut broke in. He felt his temper breaking at last; and it felt damned good. A feeling almost of exultation filled him. Here was a target he could hit. "And I have a sneaking suspicion these gentlemen didn't come here to listen to your expectations. I'm trying to tell you what we've learned so far. If you'd sit still and listen for a few minutes, you might find it unnecessary to waste time with pointless needling. Now, as I was saying—"

"Look here—" The senator started from his chair, but allowed his colleagues to pull him back and soothe him.

"—we're fairly certain we have two points of power loss to deal with, one considerably more massive than the other. The lesser of the two seems to be located quite close to the generating station, possibly in the mountainous area to the north—"

"What in the world is up there that could be drawing power from the net?" a thin, elderly fellow whom Hunnicut recognized as a state-university board member burst out, then subsided, looking embarrassed.

"We don't know. We're proceeding on the theory that it's a purely natural phenomenon—"

"How is that possible?" the senator snorted. "I seem to remember being told that this entire system is a vastly sophisticated piece of ultramodern engineering, that the whole theory behind it isn't more than five years old—"

"Nature knows nothing of our theories," Hunnicut said flatly. "The sun was shining long before we understood subnuclear physics, radioactivity was heating the earth for five billion years before the Curies. It may well be that some type of geological formation we know nothing about has the characteristic of absorbing energy in the broadcast spectrum. That theory may or may not be supported by the other findings we've developed."

"No dramatic pauses, if you please, Mr. Hunnicut!" the senator interjected into the momentary silence.

"I'll remind you that this is tentative, gentlemen." Hunnicut ignored the barb. "But at the moment, it appears that the second demand point coincides with the center of the storm that's ripping the East Coast to shreds at the moment."

"So—what does that mean?"

"As to that, Senator, your guess is as good as mine."

"Very well, what's your guess?"

"My guess," Hunnicut said slowly, staring the senator down, "is that the thing that's creating the whirlpool is drawing its power from the Pasmaquoddie station."

There was a burst of exclamations; the thin voice of the Interior Department man won out: "You're saying that someone—the Communists, perhaps—are using our power system to create this storm?"

"I said nothing about Communists. But the relationship seems indisputable."

"Poppycock!" the senator barked. "You're attempting to explain away the failure of your scheme by conjuring up imaginary menaces. Russians, manipulating the weather, eh? That's the damnedest piece of nonsense I've ever—"

"That's not what I said!"

"But you implied it!"

"I implied nothing—"

"Gentlemen!" Peacemakers were on their feet, urging the two verbal antagonists to their seats. "This wrangling is getting us nowhere," an army colonel said. "We're here to assemble data, nothing more. Let's stick to the facts."

"The facts are that I'm recommending that the transmitter be shut down immediately, until the possible correlation can be checked out," Hunnicut said.

"Preposterous!" the senator barked. "That would be a public announcement of failure!"

"Impossible," the Interior Department representative said flatly. "The entire project would be discredited by any such shutdown—to say nothing of the problems it would cause those facilities that are now operating on the broadcast system."

"Very well; you gentlemen can act as you see fit. But I'm submitting my recommendation in writing to the Secretary, personally."

"If you do, Mr. Hunnicut," the senator said, "that will be the end of a promising career."

"If I don't," Hunnicut said, "it may be the end of something considerably more important than the professional future of one underpaid government employee!"

5

The insistent *chirrr* of the muted telephone woke the President of the United States from a restless sleep. He lifted the faintly glowing receiver and cleared his throat.

"All right," he said.

"Mr. President, General Maynard is recommending immediate evacuation of the Florida Keys. Governor Cook has declared a state of emergency and requests federal disaster action."

"Winds still rising?"

"Yes, sir. Over ninety knots now. Record tides along the entire south Florida coast. Water and wind damage as far north as Hateras. No signs of any letup, according to Merritt Island."

"Tell the general to go ahead with the evacuation. Give him full armed-forces support. I don't envy him the chore."

"No, sir. I have one other item; I wouldn't have bothered you, but as long as I already have—an engineer on the Pasmaquoddie project, a man by the name of Hunnicut—"

"I remember the name, Jerry."

"Yes, sir. He's submitted a recommendation direct to Secretary Tyndall, over the heads of his direct superiors, to the effect that the power broadcast is in some way affecting the storm; making it worse, I gather. He's requesting authorization to shut down long enough to observe results, if any."

"That's a pretty extreme request, Jerry."

"Hunnicut is known as a level-headed man, sir. And he's laying his job on the line with this action. Still, as you say, it sounds fantastic."

"Check it out, Jerry. Get some other opinions—outside opinions. Don't let Bob Tyndall pressure you. Get at the facts. And see what impact this shutdown would have."

"I checked that aspect out, sir. There'd be no particular problem, except for Caine Island prison. They're on the broadcast net, as you know. And they've lost their back-up capability. The winds have knocked out the overwater cable, and their standby generators have been flooded. Without broadcast power they'd be in serious trouble."

"What about evacuation?"

"Sir, there are twelve hundred maximum-security prisoners at Caine Island."

"I see. All right, get on it and come back to me with firm recommendations by . . ." The President glanced at the glowing dial of the bedside clock. "Hell, I might as well get up and come down to the office. I'm not going to get any more sleep tonight, in any case."

The courier boat is hidden in the place Lokrien had described, a shallow gorge high in the mountains. The smooth green-gray curve of the U1-metal hull glows softly in the dark. As Gralgrathor slides down the slope in a clatter of pebbles, the entry port, triggered by the field generated by the bioprosthetics devices in his body opens to admit him. Hammer in hand, he strides along the glare-strip-lighted passage to the control compartment.

"Welcome aboard, Captain-Lieutenant," a smooth voice says from above him. He goes flat against the wall, his teeth bared; he has forgotten that the ships of Ysar speak with a man's voice.

"Commander Lokrien is not aboard at this time," the construct-voice states. "Kindly make yourself comfortable until his return. The refreshment cubicle is located—"

"Where is he?"

"I detect that you are agitated," the voice says calmly. "You are invited to make use of a tranquiling spray." There is a soft click! and a small silver tube pops from a dispenser slot beside the conn chair.

Gralgrathor snarls, swings the hammer against the plaston panel. It rebounds harmlessly.

"Attention!" the voice says sharply. "You are ordered to withdraw from the control compartment at once! This is an operational urgent command!" A sharp jolt of electricity through the floor reinforces the words. Gralgrathor

95

whirls and runs aft, slamming open each door, searching every cranny of the compact vessel.

"Where are you hiding, Loki?" he shouts. "Come out and face me, and tell me again about the needs of the empire!"

"Captain-Lieutenant, I perceive that you are in a dangerously excited state." The cybernetic voice issues from a speaker in the passage. "I must ask you to leave the vessel at once." A low-voltage shock throws him against the bulkhead; he turns and makes his way, stumbling, to the power-cell chamber door, smashes the lock with a blow; inside, ignoring repeated shocks, he takes aim at the massive conductors leading up from the coil chamber, and with all the power of his back and arms, brings the hammer down on the casing. The instantaneous blast that follows blows him into scarlet darkness.

Chapter Seven

1

Inside the big house, Falconer ushered the cab driver into a high-ceilinged room with trophy-covered oak walls, a vast granite fireplace, deep rugs, low, comfortable furniture. He poured the man a drink at a mahogany-topped bar that occupied most of one wall adjacent to glass doors that opened onto a flagstoned terrace.

"I'll be with you in about ten minutes," he said, and left the room, went up the wide, curved stairway, along the hall to a spacious bedroom. He donned a heavy cavalry-twill shirt, whipcord jodhpurs, low boots. He strapped a lightweight holster under his arm, fitted a flat pistol to it, then pulled on a dark-blue navy-issue weather jacket.

Zabisky looked around as Falconer reentered the study.

"You got some nice pieces here, mister," he said. He pointed a blunt forefinger at a tarnished cuirass and a pair of crossed pikes over the bar.

"That looks like the old Polish armor," he said. "Sixteen hundreds. It took a man to wear that stuff all day, I'll tell you."

Falconer nodded. "Indeed it did. You're interested in armory?"

"Well, you know. A guy's got to have a hobby," he said. "You got quite a collection here." His eyes roved over the array of weapons, plate armor, mail, the faded banners and scarred escutcheons. "Hey," he said, pointing

97

with his chin toward a lozenge-shaped shield bearing a design of a two-headed eagle in dark bronze. "Where'd you get that?"

"At Vienna."

"Funny. I got a old beer tankard at home, been in the family for a long time, got the same picture on it. Supposed to belonged to my ancestors. The story is, we had a king in the family, once." He laughed, glancing sideways at Falconer. "I guess it's a lot of crap, but my old great-aunt Dragica, she's a nut on genealogy, you know; she comes up with all this stuff."

"Your name was familiar," Falconer said. "You're a descendant of King John Sobieski?"

"Yeah, that was his name. You heard of him? Geez. I'm named for him."

"He was a man," Falconer said. "Taller than you, big as an ox through the chest and shoulders, fair hair, but eyes much like yours. He had the gift of laughter. He was much beloved by his men."

Zabisky stared, gave a short laugh. "You talk like you knew the guy."

"I've read of him," Falconer said shortly. "Let's go, John."

"Yeah." Zabisky followed Falconer outside; in the drive, he halted.

"Hey, mister—there's just one more thing. . . ."

Falconer turned. Zabisky took a quick step toward him, rammed a powerful right jab toward Falconer's sternum. Falconer turned half sideways, caught the wrist, brought it forward under his left arm, levered the elbow backward across his chest.

"O.K., I just wanted to check." Zabisky said.

They went along a brick walk; Falconer lifted one of the five doors on the long garage. Zabisky whistled at the gleaming shapes parked in the gloom. He walked along the line.

"A Jag XK120, an SJ Doosie, a SSK Mercedes, a Bugatti 41, ain't it? And what's that? It looks like a thirty-five Auburn . . ."

"It's a sixty-eight Auburn 866. New production."

"Man, you know your cars. Which one we taking?"

"The Auburn."

Zabisky whistled again, running a hand along the sleek lines of the car. "What's she got under the hood?"

"A Thunderbird 386-horsepower V-8."

"And I get paid too, hah? Let's go, pal. I want to see how this baby turns up."

They pulled out along the drive swiftly, noiselessly. At the road, Zabisky turned to Falconer.

"Where to?"

Falconer pointed.

"What town we headed for?"

"Just drive, John. I'll tell you when to turn." Falconer leaned back against the smooth leather seat and in ten seconds was sound asleep.

2

"The Highway Patrol found the car parked on a side street in Brooksville," Captain Brasher said. "Key in the ignition, nobody around."

"What kind of neighborhood was it?" Hardman asked.

The captain gave a lift of his khaki-epauleted shoulders. "After all, I wasn't there, I can't be expected to know every detail—"

"That's just what I do expect, Brasher! And I don't expect to wait until morning to find out what kind of car Grayle is driving now!"

The intercom buzzed; the governor jabbed the button savagely.

"Sir, Captain Lacey of the Highway Patrol on the line for Captain Brasher. Shall I—"

"Put him on." He picked up the phone, listened to clicks.

"This is Hardman at Caine Island, Captain," he said. "I'll take your report."

"Yes, sir. On the Rambler: we found it in Brooksville—"

"Yes, I know. Any leads?"

"Looks like he knocked over the watchman at the Ford car agency; it's just across the street from where the Rambler was parked. He's still out, but when he comes around he can tell us if anything's missing from the lot."

"Good. Keep me informed." The governor cradled the phone and looked across at Brasher. "He took a car from the Ford lot he was parked beside. We don't know what model or color, but we can be pretty sure it's a new one." He swiveled to look at the map of the state on the wall. "Lacey, I want you to watch I-74 and I-4, and US 19, north and south. Stop any new Ford."

"That's a pretty tall order—"

"Still—I'm ordering it!" He cradled the phone and turned to Brasher.

"I want a man on the scene—a reliable man, representing my—our—interests."

"Harmon," Brasher said at once. "He's keen, a good man—"

"I thought he was in the hospital."

"He has a headache that gives him a personal interest in nailing Grayle. They'd had run-ins before."

"Get him up there, right away."

When Brasher had left, the governor poured himself a stiff Scotch from his office bar, then keyed the intercom and called for Lester Pale. The man came in a few minutes later, looking troubled.

"Anything yet, Lester?"

"Nothing that makes any sense, sir."

"Let's have it anyway."

Lester spread papers on the edge of the desk.

"My Pentagon contact came through with a reference to a prisoner named Grayle—"

"First name?"

"Just an initial: T. This Grayle was transferred to Fort Leavenworth from Fort McNair at Washington, after a court-martial conviction for murder."

"Any details of the crime?"

"Yes, sir. The trial transcript is attached. It seems he was in an army stockade at the time of the murder."

"What motive?"

"It appears he knew the victim; other than that . . ." Lester shook his head. "Frankly, this is pretty hard reading; a poor photostat to begin with, and cramped hand-writing—"

"What do you mean, handwriting? Don't you have a copy of the official record?"

"Yes, sir," Lester said flatly. "But in eighteen-sixty-three there weren't any typewriters."

Hardman stared blankly at his aide; he reached, plucked the papers from the other's hands, scanned the sheets, made a noise in his throat.

"What the devil is this, Lester? This is an account of a Civil War trial!"

"Yes, sir. The man Grayle was a Confederate prisoner, and the man he killed was a Union officer."

"Union officer?" Hardman echoed.

"There's one discrepancy in the story, though," Lester continued in a voice that seemed on the edge of breaking. "The rumor here at Caine Island was that Grayle did the job with an ax; but according to this, he used a hammer."

3

"Let me get this straight," the guard lieutenant said softly. "Are you giving me the kill order on this pigeon?"

"Not at all." Brasher's eyes stared through the other man. "But if he's gunned down in a fire fight—with witnesses that he fired the first shot . . ."

The lieutenant nodded, touched his tongue to his lips. "Yeah," he said. "Now you're talking, sir. Blake and Weinert'll feel better when they hear—"

"They'll hear nothing, damn you! Keep this to yourself. But be damned sure you're in at the kill, understand?"

"You bet, Cap'n." The lieutenant patted the old-fashioned .38-caliber solid-slug pistol he wore at his hip. "I'll be there."

4

"We should leave the main road," Grayle said.

"We can't," the girl said decisively. "The whole road system of Florida was built to carry tourists north and south in a hurry. This was all unoccupied land just a few years ago; there isn't any network of farm roads and secondary roads like there is in most states."

"What about that?" Grayle pointed to an exit from the multilaned expressway.

"It just leads into a town. We're making good time—"

They saw the roadblock then: a pair of police cruisers parked across two of the four northbound lanes three hundred yards ahead, red flashers winking. Anne wrenched the wheel hard right, with a squeal of tires took the exit ramp.

Grayle looked back. One of the police cars was in motion, swinging in a tight turn around the central divider strip.

"They saw us."

Anne hurled the car down and out of the curving ramp, joined a wide, empty avenue glistening under the eerie blue glare of pole-mounted mercury-vapor lamps. Above high, concrete-retained banks, the fronts of ancient frame houses stared out across the traffic chasm like gaunt old men facing an open grave. A cross street was coming up; Anne braked, skidded, caught it, slammed over the curb and across the apron of a service station, missed a parked wrecker by inches, shot into the narrow mouth of a side street, sending black water sheeting. She cut the headlights, slowed to a crawl, pulled into a weed-grown driveway, reached across to tilt the rearview mirror. For a moment nothing stirred in the rectangle of glass; then light grew, became the glare of high beams, probing along the dark street. The flasher winked as the police car came slowly along the street. A spotlight beam lanced out, pushed hard shadows across the headliner. The car halted ten feet from the rear bumper of the Ford.

"Don't move." Grayle gripped the right-side door handle, twisted it silently, held it. Rain beat on the top of the car; faintly, feet squelched in mud, coming forward along the right side. As they halted, Grayle threw the door open, sending the man reeling back and down. He came out of the car in a lunge, stooped, and swept the gun from the hand of the felled policeman, threw it from him, flattened himself against the side of the car near the rear wheel. He looked at the angry, frightened face staring up at him.

"Tell your partner to throw away his gun and come around to this side," he said.

The man on the ground didn't move, didn't speak. Rain washed pink blood from a cut lip down across his face.

"Go for his feet, Charlie!" he shouted suddenly, and threw himself at Grayle in a scrambling plunge. A vivid double flash, the *boom-boom!* of a gun, from the other side of the car, whining ricochets. Grayle rounded the back of the car, straight-armed the man coming from the opposite side, sent him sprawling. He ran for the cover of the ragged junipers lining the drive, plunged through as the gun racketed again. He ran past the front of the house, ripped through a four-foot hedge, cut left, was back at the curb. One of the men was running heavily down toward the police car in the street. Grayle sprinted, reached it first, had the door open when he saw the second policeman grappling with a slim, furiously struggling figure beside the Ford. The running cop had seen Grayle; he skidded to a halt, bringing his gun up—

Grayle dived under the flash, heard the *spang!* of the solid slug against metal behind him as he took the man at knee height, felt bone break, heard the ragged scream of the man as he fell away. Grayle rolled to his feet, ran up the drive. The man by the car threw Anne from him; the slim, flat needle-pump in his hand made a harsh, rasping buzz; Grayle felt the blow of a fiery club against his chest; then he was on the man, spinning him, throwing the gun away into the darkness. He put a thumb hard into the base of the policeman's neck, dropped him. He lifted Anne, ran to the police car, tossed her onto the seat.

"Can you drive this?"

"Yes." The engine was idling. Grayle slid into the seat and closed the door; the car spun away from the curb, fishtailed, straightened out, its headlights burning a tunnel through blackness. Anne looked sideways at Grayle.

"Are you all right? I thought he shot you—"

"I'm all right."

"He couldn't have missed! Not at that distance!"

"Watch the road," Grayle said gently. He put his hand on his side; the heavy prison shirt was ripped; under it, hot blood oozed from his torn hide. Anne's eyes went to his hand. She gasped, and the car veered. "You're hurt!"

"Don't be concerned about me, Anne. We have more immediate problems—"

A voice crackled from the car radio: "Jig one to Jig nine-two-five, where's that report, Clance? Over."

Grayle lifted the microphone dangling from a hook at the center of the dash, pressed the key.

"Jig nine-two-five to Jig one," he said, holding the mike well away from his mouth and roughening his voice. "Busy; call you later."

"Clance? What was that?" The man at the other end called twice more, then switched off abruptly.

"You didn't fool him," Anne said. "They have directional gear; they know where this car is. They're tracking us right now."

They had turned into a prosperous-looking commercial street. Neon and glare signs shone through the driving downpour. A tall Sabal palm was down across the flooded street. The wind blew fallen fronds across the pavement. There were no people in sight, few cars at the curb.

Grayle picked up the map from the seat, opened it out, studied the street map on the reverse.

"There's an airfield shown here, nearby," he said. "The police and taxi copter port."

"Yes?"

"Turn left ahead. It's about a mile."

"You did say 'Police'?"

"We need an aircraft; we have little choice—"

"Grayle, I can't fly a copter."

"Perhaps I can."

"But—you can't drive a car!"

"I'm not familiar with ground vehicles, but I have considerable experience as a pilot. Do as I ask, Anne. As you said, we have no time to waste."

Anne laughed with a touch of hysteria, swung into a cross avenue toward a towering column of lights in the distance, doing a steady forty miles an hour down the center of the wide palm-lined street. A police car passed them, screaming in the opposite direction. As they swung around the periphery of a wide plaza, a second police car passed them without slowing. The avenue ran straight between wide lawns crossed by broad walks, punctuated by illuminated fountains. Ahead, the lake was blackness.

Before a low building on the left, there was movement in a courtyard. Another car emerged from a ramp and sped away. There was a lighted gate ahead. A policeman in a yellow slicker stepped from the shed to wave them through. Anne gave a gasp that was half a sob, half-laughter.

"People see what they expect to see," Grayle said. "They don't expect to see us here."

There were a dozen or more small aircraft in sight; three large fifty-passenger crosstown shuttles bearing commercial blazons, several smaller civil craft, a big police riot heli, a number of small, fast two-man machines. At the far end of the line were a pair of squat, winged VTOL craft with army markings. The headlights shone on them in turn as the car swung in a wide curve.

"Pull up there," Grayle said.

Anne pulled the car to a stop beside the first in line.

"Good-bye, Anne," Grayle started.

"You intend to leave me here to face the police alone?" Anne asked with a smile that relieved the words of accusation.

"Very well. Let's go." Grayle jumped out, glanced over the small, short-winged machine, then swung up beside the canopy; he felt over smooth metal, found a lever. The hatch opened with a soft whirring sound. As he slipped into the cockpit, Anne pulled herself up, slid gracefully into the front seat. Grayle closed the hatch, studied the array of luminous dials. He touched a button, and a cockpit light came on.

Anne turned to look back at him. "Are you sure you can fly this?"

"It shouldn't be difficult," he replied absently; he touched another button, and starters chugged; the short, wide-bladed propellers to either side flicked over jerkily. There was a burst of vapor from one engine; it caught, and a moment later the second joined in, whining up to speed. Grayle found the brake release, gave the engines a burst of power; the awkward ship rolled forward on its tricycle gear, rocking in the wind. The nose wheel, Grayle discovered, was steerable by the wheel before him. He turned sharply, passing close to the guard shack and the fence, swinging back out to face the wind howling off the lake. Again he paused to study the controls. One pair of levers ended in blunt cones, not unlike the engine nacelles and spinners. He grasped them and moved them up from horizontal to vertical. The nacelles obediently rotated. Now the propellers spun in a plane parallel to the pavement.

"Grayle—hurry! They've seen us!" Anne said. He followed the direction of her glance, saw men coming across from the gate at a run.

"Fasten your belt," he called over the shrill of the turbines. "I suspect this machine is highly unstable."

He opened the throttles; instantly the craft leaped upward, nose high, drifting backward. He righted it; the plane hurtled forward, rocking and buffeting in the wind. Lights whipped past, just beyond the stubby wingtip, dropping away. Grayle turned the craft, letting the wind carry it. The altimeter needle moved jerkily around the dial. The compass steadied on a course of 305. At an airspeed of three hundred and fifty and a groundspeed fifty knots higher, the craft raced toward the northwest.

5

"We're dealing," said the chief meteorologist, United States Weather Service, "with a cone of air approximately one mile in height and having a diameter of two miles, in rotation at the rate of one revolution each one hundred and five seconds. The rate is increasing slowly on a decreasing exponential curve and should, for all practical purposes, stabilize in another thirty hours at approximately one RPM, giving a peripheral velocity of about one hundred and ten knots."

"They're already reporting winds in excess of a hundred miles an hour all the way from West Palm Beach to Boston," one of his audience of high-ranking government officials comprising the Special Advisory Group cut in.

The weatherman nodded calmly. "Frictional forces naturally influence a large volume of air outside the nucleus of the disturbance. After stabilization, we should expect winds of over two hundred miles per hour throughout a belt about two hundred miles wide adjacent to the dynamic core, falling off at a rate of some ten knots for every hundred miles. At about one thousand miles from the center, turbulence causes a disintegration of the rotational pattern, creating randomly distributed squalls—"

"Good God, man, you're talking about a superhurricane that will devastate a quarter of the country!"

The meteorologist pursed his lips. "That's a slight exaggeration," he said carefully. "Now, as to rainfall, the estimated precipitation for the eastern portion of the country is on the order of twenty inches per twenty-four hours. I emphasize that this is an average figure—"

"Do you realize what you're saying?" another man burst out. "Twenty inches is more than some of the country gets in a year!"

"True. We can anticipate major flooding over the entire watershed. The problems involved in calculating probable runoff rates are complicated by our lack of experience in dealing with volumes of water of this magnitude, but it seems plain that the entire continental drainage pattern will be overloaded, resulting in some rather interesting erosional dynamics. For example—"

"Just a minute," a congressman interrupted. "Just how long is this rain supposed to continue?"

For the first time the weatherman looked faintly troubled. "Insofar as we've been able to calculate on the basis of limited data," he said, "there's no contraindication for indefinite continuation of the present pattern."

"What does that mean?" someone demanded.

"It means," the congressman interpreted, "that as far as they can tell, it's going to keep on raining forever."

"That's ridiculous," a Cabinet member said. "A storm draws its power from the released heat of evaporation; there's a definite limit to the size any weather disturbance can grow to. I should think it would be a relatively simple matter to calculate the theoretical limit, based on known factors of incident sunlight and so on."

"Normally, that would be true, Mr. Secretary. But the theory doesn't seem to apply in this case. You're aware that there seems to be an anomalous situation as regards displacement of seawater: the flow into the area of the whirlpool appears to be balanced by no corresponding outflow, even at great depth. The same is true of air volumes. It also seems to apply to the energy balance."

"Translation, please?" a peppery man spoke up.

"Easy, Homer," the congressman said. "Water and air are going in, and none is coming out. And the energy being expended by the storm exceeds that available from all known sources. Right, sir?"

The weatherman looked pleased. "Quite correct."

"So—what are we doing about it?"

The meteorologist's expression changed to one of mild surprise.

"Doing?" he echoed. He shook his head. "One doesn't 'do' anything about weather, Congressman. One simply observes it!"

"For God's sake, man!" A well-braided naval man spoke up. "You don't mean to tell us that we're going to just sit here and watch the country blow away—if it doesn't wash away first!"

"It's the function of my department to report the weather, Admiral—not to control it."

For several minutes the room was filled with emotional voices, all talking at once. The congressman rose and pounded the table for order.

"This is getting us nowhere, gentlemen," he said. "What about it, sir?" he addressed the meteorologist and his aides. "Is there any action—any measure at all—which you gentlemen can recommend? Seeding? Nuclear dissipation? Anything at all?"

The weathermen were shaking their heads before the question was out. There was a moment of silence.

"I heard something," an Interior Department spokesman said hesitantly. "Probably just a crank notion."

"Well?"

"One of our engineers—Hunnicut is his name, I believe—has suggested that the storm is tied in with the APU power broadcast. He claims that he's pinpointed a massive power drain right on top of the storm center. As a matter of fact, he submitted a proposal direct to the White House that the system be shut down."

"Well!" the congressman barked. "Maybe he's on to something. Let's check it out. God knows the time has come to grasp at straws."

"Well, an idea like that . . ."—the Interior man spread his hands—"can hardly be taken seriously."

"There's only one way to check it out," a White House spokesman said. "That's to shut down the system. And we can't do that." He outlined the situation as it affected the Caine Island prison.

"So—the prisoners riot in the dark. I think we can survive that."

"There's more to it than that—"

"I know—the reputations of the visionaries who poured ten billions of federal funds into the power-from-the-air scheme. But they'll just have to suffer, as I see it. I say shut down and observe the results."

"Congressman, that will take an executive order."

"Then let's get it."

There was a general mutter of agreement. The Interior man left hastily, shaking his head. The Cabinet member buttonholed the congressman.

"This is all very well, Herb," he said in a low tone. "But what if the idea's as silly as it sounds? What do we do then?"

The congressman patted the air. "Let's worry about that when we get to it, eh, Homer? Right now we'd better go see the President."

Lokrien comes up across the rocks, halts before the fire-blackened entry of the ship, from which a wisp of smoke drifts past his head.

"Xix—what happened here?"

"Sabotage by a Fleet officer," the ship's voice says. It sounds weak and thin.

"Fleet officer?" Lokrien looks out across the dark jumble of rock. "Thor—are you out there?" he calls.

There is no answer.

"I went out to look for you," Lokrien shouts into the darkness. "When I returned, your people attacked me like a pack of wild krill. Without the Y-field I'd have been killed."

A vague shape moves in the darkness. It is Gralgrathor, almost unrecognizable with half the hair burned from his head, his face blistered, his garments hanging in charred rags.

"Thor! What in the name of the Nine Gods—"

Gralgrathor leaps, swinging his hammer. Lokrien jumps back, avoiding the clumsy blow.

"Thor—have you gone mad?"

Gralgrathor snarls and moves to the attack. Lokrien avoids his rush, watches him fall.

The voice of the ship, faint and unnoticed, speaks across the darkness: ". . . fire damage to lift-coil chamber. Assault capability: negative. Defensive capability: minimal."

113

Power reserve level: critical. Category-one emergency measures now in effect. Captain-Lieutenant Gralgrathor is identified as the saboteur. . . ."

"You've wrecked my ship!" Lokrien cries. "Why? For the love of Ysar, why? Did you have to drag me down into your exile too?"

But Gralgrathor makes no answer. He struggles to rise, falls back.

"Attention, Commander!" the voice of the ship echoes across the tumbled granite, among the trees. "I will execute the traitor for his crime against the White Fleet—"

"No!" Lokrien approaches Gralgrathor. "There has to be a reason, an explanation," he pleads. "Tell me, Thor!"

Gralgrathor sways, on hands and knees. Red hate looks out of his eyes.

"I'll kill you," he snarls. "Before I die, I'll kill you."

"Commander," the ship calls. "Men approach!"

"Your mob," Lokrien says to Gralgrathor. "The same crew you set on me before—"

"I will deal with them, Commander," says the ship.

"Thor, go down to meet them, stop them, if you want to save their lives. Xix will kill anyone who comes close."

In silence, Gralgrathor climbs to his feet. Lokrien watches as he moves off like a crushed insect to disappear among the trees. Then he turns to the ship.

"Xix," he says in a broken voice. "What will we do?"

"We will survive, Commander," Xix says. "And one day we will right the wrong that was done this night."

Chapter Eight

1

"This item you asked for an analog check on, Governor Hardman," the FBI data technician said hesitantly on the grayline phone. "I'm afraid I haven't come up with anything significant. I've made runs keyed to every variable in the profile just as you asked, but I can't tie it to anything in the Main File."

"Dammit, man, here's a prisoner with no record of trial and sentencing—nothing but the mere fact of his presence here as evidence of any crime! There's got to be some explanation!"

"You've apprehended him?" the FBI man asked quickly.

"No, and the way it looks now, I'm not likely to! And if he *is* picked up, what the devil grounds do I have for holding him? I don't even know what he's supposed to have done, except by rumor!"

"It's a weirdie, all right, Governor. I'd like to help you. If you could give me some idea what it is I'm looking for—"

"I don't know! That's why I asked for the complete analysis on the few facts I have on the man—in hope you'd turn up something. I need a clue, a foothold. Dammit, in this day and age a man can't have lived a lifetime without leaving some record, some trace, somewhere!"

"Well, after all, Governor, if he's been in prison for over thirty years—"

"Nonsense! It's a case of mistaken identity. Grayle's no

115

more than forty years old at the absolute maximum. But even if he were fifty, that would still make him a federal convict at fifteen! It's nonsense!"

"Governor . . . there is one little datum that popped up. Nothing, of course, but I may as well mention it . . ."

"Well?"

The technician gave a self-conscious laugh. "The tie-in, I'm sorry to say, is more apparent than real. You recall the confusion with the Civil War trial record linked to your man? I fed that in with the rest—and the computer cross-referred to an item that came in just about three hours ago. It seems that a doctor out in Saint Louis reported removing a bullet from a man's abdomen last night. The bullet was identified as something called a minié ball, a type of solid shot used by the army in the eighteen-sixties. In other words, during the Civil War."

Hardman made a rasping noise of pure frustration. "Civil War my left elbow! What is this, Tatum, some kind of in-group joke?"

"The computer is very literal-minded, Governor."

"Any description of this chap in Saint Louis?"

"Yes, I have it here . . . six-three, two-ten, blue eyes, gray hair, reddish stubble, well set up, and extensively scarred—or rather, there seems to be a little uncertainty about that last item. The doctor reported that when he first examined the patient, the man exhibited a number of prominent scars on the face, neck, back, chest, arms—all over, virtually. But an hour later, the scars were gone. Curious, eh?"

Hardman was gripping the telephone hard. "Where is this man now?"

"That we don't know."

"Tatum, you know people. Can you put out a pickup order on this man to the Saint Louis police? Quietly? And preferably anonymously."

"You see a connection?"

Hardman laughed shortly. "Grayle is over six feet, grey-haired, red-bearded. He's reported to have shattered a pair of chrome-steel come-alongs with his bare hands, and he tore the locking bars off an armored car—also bare-handed. Either that, or he was carrying a three-quarter-ton jackhammer under his shirt. Now we have another big, gray-haired fellow out in Saint Louis whose scars miraculously heal in an hour. He was carrying a Civil War bullet. Grayle's linked to a Civil War killing. Certainly I see a connection: they're both impossible!"

"I see what you mean, Governor. I'll get right on it."

2

At the Upper Pasmaquoddie Power Station, Chief Engineer Hunnicut paced his spacious, air-conditioned, indirectly lit, soundproofed, gray-nylon-carpeted office. Beyond the wide thermopane windows the storm raged unabated. In fact, it seemed to Hunnicut, it had gained in ferocity in the last hour.

He paused at his desk—wide, highly polished, genuine mahogany—and flipped up the intercom key.

"Sam, how about that refinement on those loci?" His voice was brittle with strain.

"I was just going to call you, Mr. Hunnicut. Something odd here: the smaller one is tricky, very faint—but we've narrowed it down to a point in the mountains just north of here, within ten miles, possibly. The big one is pulling a lot of power, and we were able to cut it closer. It's about twenty miles—give or take five miles—off the west shore of Somerset Island, dead on the reported position of the storm center."

"Sam, what are the chances of an error in that placement?"

"Well, I talked to a buddy of mine at Weather in Washington about half an hour ago. He confirmed the plot on the whirlpool and swore it was accurate to inches. It hasn't moved since it was first spotted last evening. As for our fix—I'll stake my job on it. I said within five miles, but off the record I think we're within a mile. Kind of funny, eh, Mr. Hunnicut? What do you think—"

"Stand by in the main generator room, Sam. I'm coming down."

He pressed another key, spoke briskly to his secretary: "Myra, go ahead with the calls I taped earlier." He flipped off the set and left the office. In the corridor, the deep-bellied thrumming of the big generators buried in the rock below vibrated in the air, penetrating to the bones. It grew louder as he rode the lift down, passed through the intervening doors, became a solid thing as he entered the high, wide chamber almost filled by the big machines. Sam Webb was over by the big board, looking concernedly at the rows of three-inch dial faces. He turned as Hunnicut came up beside him.

"The curves are still upward," he said. "Leveling in about twenty-four hours, I'd guess. By that time, the big baby off Bermuda is going to be pulling a whale of a lot of power, Mr. Hunnicut."

"It would be, if we waited that long," Hunnicut said.

Webb frowned questioningly.

"We could shut down, Sam. We can use regular emergency procedures: shunt what we can into the Northeast Distribution Net and bleed the rest into the Erie Storage Facility. What that won't handle we can spread out over the Net links, let Central and Southeast handle it."

"Mr. Hunnicut—it's none of my business—you're the boss—but have you got an O.K. from higher up on this?"

"Don't worry, Sam. I'll take full responsibility for any orders I give."

3

The counterman at the all-night beanery waited until the quiet man in the gray slicker had seated himself and looked over the menu chalked on the dusty blackboard above the backbar before he lowered the newspaper and sauntered over. He shifted the broomstraw to the other corner of his wide mouth.

"Yeah?" he inquired.

"A man," the customer said. "Six-three, gray hair, blue eyes, husky build. Possibly scars on his face. Wearing a gray single-breasted suit with dirty cuffs. Seen him?"

The counterman's head jerked. He spat out the straw. "Who, me? I ain't seen nobody." He grabbed a yellowish rag from under the counter and began wiping the chipped Formica.

"Business is slow, eh?"

"Yeah."

"But not that slow. He was seen coming in here." The man in gray slipped a leather folder from an inside pocket and flipped it open to expose a small gold badge.

"I ain't seen nobody with no scars," the counterman said. "I don't care what some clown says he seen."

"What have you seen?"

The man lifted his bony shoulders. "Couple hackies ..." He paused.

"Go on."

"There was a mug with gray hair, you know, premature like, big bimbo. But a kid, young, no scars on him; hell, he prob'ly don't even shave."

"When was he in?"

"A couple hours ago. Hell, how do I know?"

"Any idea where he was going when he left here?"

"What do you think I am, an information bureau? I

don't know the guy, never seen him before. I'm gonna ask him where he goes next?"

"Answer the question."

"No, I don't know where he was going."

"He left on foot, or he had a car waiting?"

"He . . . didn't have no car."

The man in gray smiled gently. "You sure about that?"

"Maybe he picked up a hackie here. Yeah, I remember now. He come in here to tap a hackie was eating here. Tried to start trouble. I hadda throw the both of 'em out."

"Where did he want to go?"

"New Jersey, I guess. He said something about Princeton."

The man in gray nodded and stood.

"Thanks very much, Mr. Schutz," he said. He paused at the door and glanced back. "By the way—the business with the blackboard is cute—but I think you'd better close your book down. The cops are on to it."

The counterman's look followed him as he turned up his collar and stepped back out into the driving rain.

4

"It's certainly worth a try, Mr. President," Congressman Doberman said solemnly. "The Caine Island aspect of the thing is unfortunate, but in light of the situation—"

"If there's a legitimate technical basis for the decision to shut down the power broadcast, I'll do it, Herbert. What I'm questioning is the soundness of the proposal." The President looked at his special assistant. "What about it, Jerry?"

"Sir, Hunnicut himself is the leading authority in the field of broadcast power. The technical people I've coordinated with are all either students of his or his former teachers. All of them have the greatest respect for his judgment."

"Now, just a minute, Jerry," Secretary Tyndall cut in. "I have a few scientists of my own, I'll remind you. On my staff, that is—"

"What do *they* advise, Bob?" the President put in smoothly.

"They assure me that the idea is fantastic, Mr. President! A piece of hysteria, pure and simple! I'm not saying this scheme was set in motion by antitransmission forces, mind you, but if it had been, it couldn't have been better planned to undermine congressional confidence in the future of broadcast power!"

"All right, Bob, I understand your problem. You can set your mind at rest. No one's going to blame you—"

"It's more than that, Mr. President," Doberman said, "It's not face-saving I'm concerned about now—not entirely, at least. A thing like this can be the straw that knocks the program out for twenty years. We can't afford that. We need APU—"

"All right, Bob, I believe you. And I trust you'll believe me when I say I'm with you. But at the moment we're facing a grave situation. If we have the power to avert disaster, there's no question that we must do so."

The Secretary nodded reluctantly.

"Very well, Jerry. Don't bother with channels. Get the power station on the line, direct."

The aide spoke quietly into the grayline phone. The others waited in silence.

"Mr. Hunnicut? This is the White House calling ... Yes, the White House—Mr. Hunnicut, personally, please ..." Jerry paused, listening. His eyebrows went up.

"One moment," he cut in sharply. "Who is this speaking, please? Mr. Webb? Mr. Webb, I'm calling for the President. You are—please don't interrupt, Mr. Webb—you are instructed to shut down power broadcast immediately, until further notice. I repeat, you are instructed to shut down at once. This will be confirmed by TWX immediately. That's correct, Mr. Webb. Thank you." Jerry cradled the phone. The President was looking at him questioningly.

"Power is off, Mr. President," Jerry said, looking uncomfortable.

The President nodded. "That's done, gentlemen. Thank you for coming over. Please keep me closely informed of any results—and, Bob, I'd appreciate it if you'd speak to Ray Cook personally, offer any assistance we can give. I suppose it's possible to get some sore of portable power in to Caine Island . . ."

After the others had left, the President looked at his aide with a faint smile.

"Mr. Hunnicut was a mite impatient, was he, Jerry?"

"His deputy was trying to tell me something, Mr. President," Jerry said, looking his chief in the eye. "I didn't catch what it was."

The President nodded. "You're a good man, Jerry," he said.

"You're a good man yourself, Mr. President."

5

"I got through to the White House, all right, Mr. Hunnicut," Sam Webb said. "Or rather . . ." He shook his head, but the dumbfounded expression remained on his face. "They got through to me. It was a presidential order to pull the transmitters off the line."

Hunnicut smiled slightly, his eyes on the panel before him. The sound of the generators had changed; distantly, heavy relays could be heard, slamming closed. Needles nodded and wavered on the big dials. Hunnicut's smile faded, was replaced by a frown. A side door burst open, and simultaneously the telephone clanged harshly.

"Mr. Hunnicut! Big trouble! The transmitters have switched themselves back on again! The whole relay bank has gone nuts! Circuits are welding themselves, fuses are arcing over—"

Webb grabbed up the phone. "Yes—all right, we know about it, we're on the way!" He slammed the instrument down, at a run followed the others from the room.

Ten minutes of frenzied effort by a dozen engineers yielded no result. Power continued to pour from the generators into the giant transmitting coils.

"Look at this," a man called from a repeater board. "We're still being drawn on for a full load—but only two stations are drawing power—" His voice faltered. "And those two are . . . are . . ."

"I don't get it, Joe! What the hell does it mean?"

"Simple," Hunnicut answered. "The outlaw demand points are still drawing power—our total output, now. And they're going to keep on drawing power whether we like it or not!"

6

Max Wiston, number P978675-45, who had, three weeks before, completed the first decade of a life sentence to Caine Island for rape and murder, was sitting on his bunk in cell 911-m-14 when the lights went out. At the same instant, the music of Happy Dan and his Radio Folks faded; the soft hiss of air from the ventilator died into silence.

For all of ten seconds, Max sat unmoving, eyes wide open against the darkness, ears straining for a sound. Then a yell sounded from somewhere nearby:

"Hey, what's with the lights? I'm tryn'a read!" The next instant, a bedlam of calls and yells had broken out. Max rose and groped across the cell, hands outstretched. He put his face against the bars; no faintest glimmer of light was visible anywhere. There were screams mingled with the yells now; to a latent claustrophobe, the total absence of light could be as confining as a tomb.

Max stood by the cell door, his mind racing. He had known from the moment that the sentence was pronounced on him that he would never spend the rest of his life in prison. He was a man who had lived out of doors, on the water, gone in boats, known the open sea. One day he'd regain the life that the bitch and slut had taken away from him. In the meantime, he would go along quietly, pretend to accept his fate—and wait. And one day his chance would come.

And now it had. He knew it. He could smell it in the air. All he had to do was think, make the right moves, not panic, not louse it up. Think. Think, Max.

Lights off, air off, radio off. O.K. No power. There was a storm, lines were down. . . . But there was something about switching to a new system, broadcast power. Maybe that was it. It hadn't worked out; new stuff was always developing kinks. So all right, the details didn't matter, the point was—no power. Meaning no alarm bells, no intruder circuits, no timed locks on the cellblock interlock.

. . .

A dazzling thought entered Max's head. Gingerly, delicately, he reached through the bars, felt along the cold metal for the outer manual latch. Gently, he grasped it; carefully, he turned it.

The door swung open.

For a moment Max stood in the darkness, smiling. Then he stepped out, paused to orient himself, and started toward the guard post at the end of the passage.

7

"That's right," the service-station attendant said. "Some car, you wouldn't forget that one in a hurry. Two men in it; the driver was a rough-looking character, flat nose, bullet-headed, you know. Had on a yellow-and-brown mackinaw. The other guy . . . well, I don't know. He was asleep, didn't say anything. What I figured, he owned the car, and this other guy was his chauffeur—only he didn't look much like my idea of a chauffeur. Maybe—hey! Maybe the guy stuck him up, took his car. Maybe the guy . . ." The attendant swallowed. "Maybe the guy was dead!"

"If he were dead," the man in the tan car inquired, "why would the murderer carry him around with him?"

"Yeah, it don't make sense. Anyway, now I remember the guy said something." The attendant sounded disappointed. "Just as they were pulling out."

"Do you remember what he said?"

The man lifted his cap to scratch his head. "Something about . . . 'We're getting close. Steer a little more to the east. . . .' Something like that."

"And this was how long ago?"

"Heck, not more'n fifteen, twenty minutes."

"Thanks." The man in the tan car pulled away from the pumps. As he accelerated to join the fast lane, he was speaking urgently into a microphone.

8

When Falconer woke again, the big car was bumping over a rough-surfaced road. The wind was still beating at the car, but the rain had slackened perceptibly. He sat up, instantly alert.

"Where are we, John?"

"West of Saint Paul a few miles," Zabisky said. "I had to get off the interstate."

"Why?"

"You said to steer east. What am I going to do, cut out cross-country?"

Falconer nodded. "I'm hungry," he said. "Stop at the first eating place you see, John."

"Geez, you can sure pack it in, brother! Sleep and eat, that all you do, fer Chrissakes?"

"I'm making up for lost time, John. I've been off my feed, you might say."

"There ain't no eating joints along here. Cripes, the lousy road ain't even maintained. I ain't seen a house for ten miles. And this lousy rain ain't helping any."

Zabisky hunched over the wheel, staring out into the rain, sweeping in almost horizontal gusts across the road. "Anyways, there ain't much traffic. Most people got better sense, in this weather."

Falconer glanced at the outside-mounted rearview mirror, saw a flash of lights, far back.

"How long has that car been behind us?"

The driver looked up at his mirror. "Geez, it beats me. I ain't seen him."

Two miles farther, the car behind had closed the gap to half a mile.

"Speed up a little," Falconer said.

"Hey," Zabisky said. "Is that guy tailing us, or what?" He looked sideways at his employer. "What is this caper, anyway, mister? I told you I don't want to get mixed in nothing shady."

"We're doing nothing illegal, John. See if you can gain on him."

"I'm doing all I can, fer Chrissakes! Fifty in this soup is like a hundred and ten!"

"He seems to be bettering that."

Zabisky swore and accelerated. The low-slung car veered from side to side on the single-lane road, bucking the squall winds. Rounding a turn, it broke away, went into a tail-wagging slide before the driver wrenched it back into the center of the road.

"Ha! Our pal back there don't like the pace," he said.

His spirits seemed to be rising under stress. The Auburn roared ahead on a long straightaway. The speedometer needle reached sixty, crept toward seventy. Belatedly, the headlights of the car behind them appeared around the bend.

"Oh-oh," Zabisky said, watching in the mirror. "He's trying to straighten out the curve—" The following lights veered suddenly, swept across treetops, and went out.

"He bought it," Zabisky said. "Scratch one tail."

"We'll have to go back," Falconer said.

"Hah? I thought—"

"Somebody may be bleeding to death, John."

Zabisky brought the car to a halt.

"Who were they, anyway, cops?" he asked.

"I don't know, John."

"Why they tailing us?"

"I don't know that, either."

"For a smart guy there's a lot you don't know."

"Nevertheless, I'm telling you the truth. Let's get moving, John."

Muttering, Zabisky backed, turned, drove back along the narrow road at thirty. The headlights showed up a tan-colored car upside down in the drainage ditch. The front wheels were still spinning slowly.

"Flipped neat," Zabisky said, pulling over so as to illuminate the wreck with his headlights. Falconer opened the door and stepped out into the gusting rain, went across the strip of sodden turf to the car. It rested on its top in a foot of muddy, swirling water. Inside it a man was slumped against the cracked glass of the windshield like a bundle of old clothing. His face was half under water.

"Cripes, the poor boob'll drown," Zabisky shouted over the drumming of the storm. Falconer stepped down into the water and tried the door handle. It was jammed tight. He twisted harder. The metal yielded, broke with a sharp sound.

"Geez, the cheap metal they use these days," Zabisky said. He splashed around the front of the car. "We got troubles," he called. "She's tight against the bank. This door ain't opening, no matter what!"

Falconer felt along the edge of the door. It was sprung sufficiently to allow him to insert his fingertips under it. He pulled gently. The doubled metal flange folded back without budging the door.

"Hey, that guy inside ain't going to last much longer," Zabisky called. "That water's coming up fast! Maybe we can bust out the windshield—but I'd hate to see the mug's face after we finish. . . ."

Falconer went to one knee, exploring the edge of the door below water level. It was twisted in the frame, exposing one corner. He thrust a finger through, levered the door outward far enough to get a two-handed grip. He braced his feet and pulled. The metal bent slowly, then folded back before springing open. Falconer reached inside, eased the injured man out onto the muddy bank. He was breathing noisily through his mouth. Water ran from his nose. He coughed, then breathed easier. Except for a swelling on his forehead, he seemed to be uninjured.

As Falconer stood, he caught sight of Zabisky's face. The swarthy skin looked yellowish in the harsh beam of the headlights; the stubble on the big chin stood out like greasepaint. He was shaking his head in emphatic denial.

"I never seen nothing like that," he said, staring at the ruined door. The latch dangled from the torn metal of the jamb. "I seen strong guys, but nothing like that. What are you, mister?" His eyes met Falconer's.

"I'm a man with strong hands, John. That's all."

"Uh-uh," Zabisky said. "Nobody's got hands like that —" He broke off as shadows moved. He whirled, almost losing his balance on the slippery slope. A car was approaching from the south. Falconer went flat against the bank. The oncoming car slowed, halted twenty feet away. A spotlight speared out to highlight Zabisky.

"Hold it right there," a voice called. Doors opened and slammed. Two men came forward, bulky in shiny rain gear. Zabisky stood with his hands held clear of his sides, not moving, watching them. One halted ten feet away, holding a heavy pistol trained on the driver's chest. The other came up from the side, reached under the mackinaw to frisk the man.

"Hell, this ain't the guy," the man with the gun said. Light winked on the badge on his cap.

The other man was looking at the overturned car. "What happened?"

"He spun out," Zabisky said. "The damn fool tried to take the curve at seventy—in this soup!"

"Yeah? Where do you tie in?"

" . . . I come back to see to the guy."

The man who had searched him pushed him, staggering him. "I like it better you ambushed him. What did you do, shoot out a tire? Or feed him a pill through the windshield?"

"Where's your partner?" the other man said. "Talk it up, Hunky. We don't like cop-killers a lot, even federal-cop killers."

"He ain't dead—" Zabisky started and was cut off by a short, powerful right jab to the midriff. He bent over, hugging himself.

"How do you like that, Roy, a glass gut," the cop with the gun said.

"He's laid out over there," Zabisky grunted, forcing himself upright.

The unarmed cop went over, looked down at the man lying on the shoulder.

"He's breathing," he called. He came back to stand before Zabisky. "Why'd you pull him out?"

Zabisky squared his shoulders. He stared into the light at the shadowed face of the policeman.

"Go knit a sweater, copper," he said. This time, as the cop's fist shot out, Zabisky half-turned away, caught the wrist, yanked the man to his chest, levering the elbow across his ribs.

"You," he said to the other cop. "Drop it or I fix your partner so he has to drink his beer through a straw."

The gun held steady on Zabisky. The cop twisted his mouth in a grinlike grimace. "What if I say tough lines, Rube? What's an arm to me, compared to a slug in your kneecap—especially if it's some other guy's arm?

Zabisky backed, dragging the policeman with him. "You better be good with the rod, copper. Otherwise your pal stops the slug."

"Could be, Rube. Let's find out." The cop took up a pistol-range stance, body turned sideways, gun arm straight out, left hand on hip, leaning back for balance. He sighed carefully, still grinning—

Falconer came up out of the ditch in a rush, swept up the gunner, and in a single movement threw him clear across the road to crash through unmowed brush, sending water splashing high. He gripped the coat-front of the other man, lifted him, shook him gently.

"See to this man," he said, nodding toward the accident victim. "Come along, John. We've wasted too much time here." He dropped the policeman, who sprawled where he had been deposited.

Zabisky hesitated a moment, then went quickly to the car, slid in under the wheel. He watched Falconer get in, slam the door. "Mister—I must be nuts, but I kind of like your style." He started up, pulled off down the wet road with an acceleration that pressed both men back against the solid leather seats.

9

Grayle watched the instruments, holding the small air-craft at ten thousand feet, the airspeed at three hundred and forty. He paid no attention to the compass. Sitting in the seat before him, Anne stared out at the night, as opaque as black glass. The ship bucked and pitched, dropped abruptly, surged upward, rocked. The whine of the engines was an unending scream, like a cat in a fire.

Grayle was frowning, his head tilted. At the edge of hearing there was a sound—a faint, rumbling undercurrent to the background din of the roaring turboprops. It grew steadily, became a roar. Off the port wingtip, slightly ahead, an orange glow appeared, winking fitfully, sliding closer. A point of green light became visible, then a white one, above and behind it. Vaguely, Grayle made out the metallic shape behind them.

"It's a jet fighter plane," Anne gasped. "It's pacing us."

Slowly, the jet moved ahead. Just before it reached the limit of visibility, it banked up, showing its port-wingtip light, and whipped directly across the course of the smaller plane. Grayle fought the controls as the craft leaped and bounced in the slipstream. Anne pointed. A second jet had appeared on the right.

"Hold on," Grayle said. He threw the control stick sideways and applied full rudder, at the same time cutting the throttles and rotating the engines to the vertical. He feathered the propellers as the small plane veered sharply to the left and dropped like a stone. The altimeter wound down the scale, to nine thousand feet, eight, seven . . .

At four thousand feet, he engaged the props, applied power. The engines shrieked; the fall slowed. He leveled off at two thousand feet.

Grayle worked the controls, rotating the nacelles for

forward thrust. For half a minute the plane streaked eastward in total darkness. Then the plane leaped as solid sound erupted around them. With a long, shattering roar, one of the jets flashed past. In the brief glow of its tailflame, wisps of fog whipped and tattered, ragged sheets of rain whirled, dissipating. Grayle put the nose down and poured on full power. At under one thousand feet he leveled off again. For an instant, through a break in the enveloping mist, he caught a glimpse of a vague shape flashing past below. He pulled the nose up, throttled back, glanced at the altimeter; it indicated nine hundred feet.

"Anne! On what principle does this altitude indicator operate? Reflected radiation? Or—"

Something dark loomed up before them; Grayle whirled to Anne, caught her in his arms, twisted to set his back against the padded panel as with a rending, smashing impact the plane struck.

"Emergency measures must be undertaken at once," the ship says. "No time must be lost in returning to the battle line. I am operating on Final Emergency Reserves now. Unless my power coil is reenergized promptly, I will soon drop to a sub-alert state."

"It's going to take time, Xix," Lokrien says. "I can't leave you lying here exposed, to be picked over by every wandering souvenir hunter who comes past. Can you quarry enough stone to conceal yourself?"

"The energy expenditure will leave me drained," the machine says. "But I compute that it can be done."

Lokrien gathers a few items into a pack, leaves the ship.

"Commander," the voice of Xix calls.

Lokrien looks back at the sleek-lined hull.

"I will be unable to speak after this expenditure of energy. Farewell. Remember that I will be waiting beneath the rock, confident of your return."

"You were a good ship, Praxixytsaran the Ninth. You will be again, one day."

Behind Lokrien, energy thundered. Bolts of blue-white fire rayed out to cut and lift great slabs of granite. When silence fell, nothing was to be seen but the tumbled rock, swathed in settling dust.

Chapter Nine

1

"Let me get this straight, Mr. Hunnicut," the President said carefully. "You're telling me that the sole result of the shutdown of the power broadcast is the plunging of seven federal installations into darkness? That two unauthorized and unidentified demand points are continuing to draw power?"

"That's about it, sir. Six of the installations are on emergency power or back on the New England Net—all but Caine Island—"

"Perhaps I'm tired, Mr. Hunnicut. How can these two bootleg receivers continue to draw power if you're no longer generating power?"

"Sir, that's the point I've been trying to explain. The station is still generating—and still broadcasting. When I shut down transmission—or tried to—the breakers arced over, welded the circuits open. I'm broadcasting whether I like it or not—and the same goes for the generators. I can't shut them down. The last man I sent in to manually disconnect is in the infirmary now, undergoing artificial respiration. We can't even get into the generator room. The whole thing is hot."

"Mr. Hunnicut, it appears to me matters at your station have gotten badly out of hand!"

"Mr. President, as chief engineer here I take full responsibility—but what's going on is abnormal—fantastically so! I don't pretend to understand it—but I

can assure you that this is more than just a simple malfunction. Someone—or something—is manipulating the
station—"

"Mr. Hunnicut, this it not the time to slide off into
mysticism! I want the broadcast of power from your station terminated at once, by any means at your command.
I hope that's quite clear?"

"Yes, sir, but—"

"That's all, Mr. Hunnicut." The President's face was
dark with anger as he racked the phone. He swiveled on
the men standing beside his desk.

"General," he addressed a compactly built officer in
army green, "how long will it take you to move a battalion
of troops into the Upper Pasmaquoddie station?"

"Two hours from the moment you so order, sir."

"Better get moving, General." He turned to a lean,
white-haired man in self-effacing gray. "Mr. Thorpe, have
the personnel you've selected stand by to cooperate with
the army as we discussed. And in the meantime, let me
know the instant your instruments indicate that my instructions have been complied with." The physicist
nodded and scurried away. The President looked at the
Secretary of the Interior, pale and owlish in the pre-
dawn.

"Funny—I wasn't at all sure that shutting down the
broadcast was the correct course, in spite of Mr. Hunnicut's persuasiveness—but now that Mr. Hunnicut seems to
have changed his mind, I'm damned if I'm going to
change mine!"

2

Outside the office of the Governor, Caine Island Federal
Penitentiary, a portable, five-KW generator chugged stolidly, powering a string of wan lights hastily rigged along
the corridor. Inside the office, the governor gripped the

telephone until his knuckles paled. He was shouting, not solely because of the booming of the storm beyond the thick walls.

"Possibly you still haven't grasped the situation here, Governor Cook! There are twelve hundred and thirty-one maximum-security federal prisoners housed in this facility, which is now totally without power and light! The PA system is inoperative. My guard force is scattered all over the prison, without light or instructions. Incidentally, the walls here are rather thick; with the air-conditioning equipment inoperative, the air is rapidly growing foul. At the time the power was cut, three hundred of these men were in the dining hall; over two hundred were at their duty posts in various parts of the facility. By the grace of God, almost seven hundred of them were secured in their cells. They're there now—in total darkness. However, the locks in the prison are electrically operated. When the power failed, they automatically went to the open position. When the men discover that—well, I leave the results to your imagination."

As Hardman paused for breath, the voice of the governor of the state of Florida spoke calmly: "I understand the situation, Jim, and believe me, this step wouldn't have been taken had there been any alternative—"

"You sound as though the power were cut intentionally!"

"It was necessary to shut down the transmitter, Jim. The President personally notified me, and believe me, the reasons he gave—"

"Damn the reasons he gave! Unless I have power here in an hour, Caine Island will be the scene of the worst outbreak of prison violence in penal history! I'm sitting on a powder keg with the fuse lit—"

"That's enough, Jim!" the state governor cut in sharply. "I have my instructions, you have yours. You're in charge of Caine Island; take whatever action is necessary to keep matters under control. That's what you're there for!"

"Now, look here, Governor—" Hardman's voice faded. He was talking into a dead receiver. He slammed the instrument down, swiveled to stare across the dim-lit office at Lester Pale. In the absence of the hum of the air circulators, the wail and boom of the storm seemed ready to tear the walls away.

"He hung up on me! After telling me that the power system was deliberately shut down! And *I'm* supposed to keep matters under control, he says!"

"Sir, I've managed to contact a dozen or so of the guard force, including Lieutenant Trent. He's issued hand torches to the men, and they're out rounding up as many others as they can find. In a few minutes we should have the majority assembled in the barracks—"

"And then what? We huddle here and wait for the prisoners to realize they have the freedom of the prison?"

"Lieutenant Trent is standing by for your orders, sir," Pale said carefully.

Hardman rubbed his hands up and down across his face, then sat erect.

"Thanks, Lester," he said. "I'm through making a fool of myself now, I hope. All right, we have a situation on our hands. Tell Trent to come up. I suppose our best bet is to concede the entire cell complex and establish ourselves here in the Admin wing. We should have enough men to control access . . ." He stopped talking, cocked his head. In the distance there was a faint popping sound.

"Gunfire!" Lester whirled to the door as it burst open. A man in guards' blue slammed halfway across the room before he came to a halt, breathing raggedly. He held a pistol in his right hand, pressing the side of the gun against his left shoulder. Blackish-red blood ran down his wrist and made a blot on his sleeve.

"My God, Governor," he blurted. "They've busted out; they shot the lieutenant, and—"

"I'll tell the rest," a hoarse voice said. A tall, rangy man in prison uniform, with weatherbeaten skin and stiff gray hair, came in through the open door. The guard-issue gun in his hand was pointed carelessly toward Hardman. The guard whirled with an inarticulate sound, bringing the gun around—

The tall prisoner twitched the gun to cover him, squeezed the trigger. There was a sharp *whac-whac!* The sound of the dope pellets hitting flesh was clearly audible. The guard took a step back with rubbery legs which folded suddenly. He hit the rug hard and lay still.

"I'm not here to mess around, Governor," Max Wiston said. "Here's what I want from you. . . ."

3

Grayle awoke with his face in icy water, the taste of mud in his mouth. For a timeless moment his mind groped for orientation: listened for the twang of bows, for the boom of cannon, the crackle of small-arms fire; for war cries, or the screams of the wounded, the clash of steel on steel, the thud of horses' hooves. . . .

But there was only the beating of the rain, hitting the mud with a sound like the rattle of muffled drums. Grayle sat up. Pain stabbed at his ribs.

The girl lay across his chest, unconscious. He touched her face: it was cold as ice.

It took Grayle ten minutes to lever torn metal aside, extricate the girl from the shattered craft, and carry her across a furrowed quagmire to the inadequate shelter of the trees which the lightning flashes revealed.

He saw the path taken by the plane after it had struck the crown of a tall oak, plowed its way through massed foliage shedding wings and empennage in the process, to impact in a plowed field. It was a miracle the girl had survived.

He was forced to lie down then. The rain fell, the wind moaned in the trees. . . .

Lights, and men's voices. Grayle got to his feet with difficulty, feeling broken ribs grate. A line of lights showed on a ridge half a mile distant: parked vehicles, he guessed. The lights were moving across the field toward him. He thrust aside the breath-stopping pain, forced his mind to focus on the situation: the path of the small craft had been followed on radar, no doubt—but they couldn't be sure whether he had landed safely, crashed, or flown on at treetop level. And that, perhaps, gave him a chance —if he moved quickly.

He bent over Anne, feeling over her for apparent injuries. There were many small cuts and abrasions, but it was impossible to say if she were seriously hurt. She needed medical help, quickly. He looked across toward the approaching lights—and at other lights, advancing now from the opposite direction. They had thrown a cordon around the area, were closing the noose from all sides. Time was running out. He must slip through them now, or not at all.

He scooped the unconscious girl up in his arms, picked a direction in which the lights seemed more widely spaced, and set off across the boggy ground, keeping his course between two lights. Once he dropped low as the beam of a powerful light traversed the field; but the same light showed him a drainage ditch marked by a growth of weeds. He angled across to it, slid down into knee-deep, muddy, swirling water. He flattened himself against the bank as two men passed by a few feet above, one on each side of the ditch. He followed the ditch for another hundred feet, then left it and altered course forty-five degrees to the right, toward the road.

He came up onto the pavement fifty yards behind the

last of the three cars in line, moved up, keeping to the ditch. Two men in rainproofs stood in the middle of the road between the first and second cars in line. Both carried rifles under their arms. Grayle came level with the last car, a four-door sedan with police markings and a tall antenna. The courtesy light glared as he opened the front door, slid Anne onto the seat. Her head lolled on her shoulder. Pink blood seeped down her wet face. Her breathing was regular but shallow.

Something on the back seat caught Grayle's eye: a snub-nosed sub-machine gun. There was also a double-barreled shotgun, boxes of ammunition, and a web belt hung with fragmentation grenades. Grayle caught up the belt, strapped it on.

There was a shout; the two men in the road were running toward the car. Grayle crossed the ditch, came up against a barbed-wire fence; he broke the strands with his hands and ran.

Half a mile from the road, he paused, raised his head, pivoting slowly, as if searching the wind for a scent. Then he set off at a steady run to the west-northwest.

4

Zabisky slowed as the headlights of the Auburn picked up a dark shape blocking the road ahead. He halted twenty feet from a big olive-drab half-track pulled across the narrow pavement. A man came forward, swinging a lantern; Zabisky lowered the window.

"Road's closed," the man said. He wore a military-type steel helmet and carried a slung rifle.

"What's the matter, road washed out?" Zabisky inquired.

"Convoy coming through," the man said. He huddled in his green slicker, water dripping from the helmet rim.

"Say, that's a wild car you got there. What is it, one of them foreign jobs?"

"Naw—made in Oklahoma. Listen, bud, we got to get through, see. We're on like important business."

The man shook his head, shifted the rifle to the other shoulder. "Nothing doing. You got to go back to Pineville, take state-road eleven—"

"We got no time for that—"

"Never mind, John," Falconer said. He leaned across. "How long will the road be closed, soldier?"

"Beats me, mister."

"What's going on?"

"Hell, who tells us anything? We get called out in the middle of this lousy storm, and—"

"O.K., knock it off, dogface." Another man had come over from the side of the road, a big fellow with a staff sergeant's stripes on his helmet. "What do you think this is, a Boy Scout jamboree?" He turned a black-browed look on the car and its occupants. "All right, you been told. Now get that heap turned around and get out of here before I have to get tough."

Zabisky gave the sergeant a long look.

"How about it, Mr. Falconer," he said loudly. "You want me to call your pal the general on the car phone?"

Falconer smiled slightly. "That won't be necessary, John." He had been glancing at the map. "Sergeant, it's a long way back to route eleven, and it doesn't seem to be going in the right direction—"

"Things are tough all over. Now, pull out of here like I told you—and you can call your pal the general and tell him I said so!"

Falconer opened his door and stepped out. The headlights threw a tall shadow across the curtain of rain as he came around the front of the car. The sergeant waited, his thumbs hooked in the pistol belt around his stomach. Falconer came up to him and without pausing drove his fist in a six-inch jab into the man's belly. The sergeant made an explosive sound and doubled over, fell to his knees. The soldier behind him gave a yell, fumbled his rifle from his shoulder in time for Falconer to catch it, twitch it away, and toss it into the ditch. Then he stepped in and slammed a short right hook to the startled lad's jaw. He tumbled down against the side of the car.

"Hey, you didn't need to slug the kid," Zabisky said. He had scrambled out of the car and grabbed the sergeant's pistol from his belt.

"A nice bruise on the jaw will help him when he talks to his C.O.," Falconer said. "Let's go." He started toward the big vehicle blocking the road.

"Hey—where you going?" Zabisky called.

"This is as far as we can go by ordinary car," Falconer said. "We were lucky to find better transportation waiting for us."

"Are you kidding, brother, talking about heisting a tank off the army—"

"You don't need to come along, John. Take the car and go back. But I suggest you abandon it at the first opportunity. The sergeant will give a detailed description of it as soon as he catches his breath."

Zabisky stared at him. "Why not tell me what this is all about? The whole thing is nuts—and this is the nuttiest item yet!" He jerked a thumb at the half-track.

Falconer shook his head. "Good-bye, John," he said. "I'm grateful for your help—"

Zabisky made a throwing-away motion. "Forget it," he said. "I told you I was in with you; I ain't quitting now."

Seated in the armored vehicle, Falconer looked over the panel, pressed the starting button. The big engine roared to life. He put it in gear, rolled forward, down into the ditch, up the other side, flattening a fence. He corrected course slightly, then settled down to steering the big machine up across sloping ground to the dark mass of the hills ahead.

5

Chief Engineer Daniel Hunnicut, his operations chief, Sam Webb, and two maintenance engineers stood in the brilliantly lit passage outside the switch-gear room of the Pasmaquoddie Power Sation. They were dressed in heavy rubber suits, gauntlets, and boots; each carried breathing apparatus. Hunnicut held a black, waxed carton firmly gripped to his chest. The engineers clutched coils of heavy wire. Tools were belted about their waists.

"I don't know how much time we'll have," Hunnicut said into the lip mike inside his breathing helmet. "It's hotter than the main bearings of hell in there. You all know what to do. No waste motion, no false moves. We place the charges, fix detonators, and get out. Any questions?"

The three men shook their heads.

"Then let's go." Hunnicut undogged the heavy door, swung it outward. A blast of light and heat struck at him, scorching even through the insulated suit. At once, the cooling units went into high-speed operation. The chief engineer led the way across the high-ceilinged room, past a gray-bright patch of solidified metal snaking across the floor to the base of the main breaker bank. He placed the carton on the floor; the wax was melting, trickling down the sides. His fingers in the thick gauntlets were clumsy, tearing away the paper wrappings. He lifted out the cigar-shaped charges of explosive, linked together in clusters of four, handed them to Webb, who swiftly inserted them at the previously selected points around the base of the massive apparatus. One of the engineers began attaching linking wires. The other busied himself laying a heavy cable across the floor.

"That's all of them," Hunnicut said. Webb nodded, tucking the last charge in place. The engineers linked up their wires, rose to their feet, looking to Hunnicut.

"Out," he said. The three men went past him to the door. The two engineers passed through into the corridor. Webb paused to glance back. He froze, pointed past Hunnicut. The latter turned. A coil of smoke was rising from the insulated wire attached to the lowest cluster of explosives. Hunnicut took a step toward it. Webb yelled, jumped after his chief as the wire burned through. The charge dropped to the floor. Hunnicut took a quick step, bent to pick up the smoking charge—

The men in the passage were thrown from their feet by the terrific, booming blast. Acoustical panels dropped from the ceiling. Through the dust boiling from the doorless opening to the switch-gear room, they caught a glimpse of a tattered thing of rags that fell away from the scorched and shattered wall opposite the entry.

Later examination identified Webb by the fillings in a surviving jaw fragment. No recognizable portion of Hunnicut was ever recovered.

Power continued to flow from the generators to the great antenna arrays of the Upper Pasmaquoddie Power Station.

For two weeks Gralgrathor has lain on a bed of stretched hides in the great hall of Björnholm, taking no food, swallowing only the mixture of wine and water that the old crone Siv presses on him before she and the other serving women perform the daily ritual of stripping away the dried, salt-impregnated cloths from the massive burn areas, tearing away along with them the day's accumulation of dead tissue, after which they smear reeking bearfat over him and rebandage him.

On the fifteenth day, he rises for the first time. The servants find him on the floor and lift him back to his bed. Two days later, he walks unaided to the door. Thereafter, he walks a little each day, swinging his arms, stretching the healing skin until the sweat of pain stands across his forehead. During the following days he practices with his weapons until he has regained a measure of his former skill. In the evenings, he roams the hills with the hound Odinstooth at his heels. During this time he says no more than a dozen words a day. He tolerates no reference to his dead wife and child, or to the were-demon who slew them on his doorstep.

A month has passed when Gralgrathor climbs the steep escarpment to the ravine where the boat had lain. He finds a vast crater of broken rock, already overgrown with wild berry vines. He stands, looking down at it for a long time. Then he makes his way back to his hall.

The next day he calls his household together and makes distribution of his lands and possessions among his servants. With only the aging Hulf as companion, and carrying only a leather-thonged hammer as weapon, he sets off on foot along the shore to the south.

Chapter Ten

1

Three men sat in a staff car parked beside the road opposite the exotic-looking civilian car abandoned by the hijackers. In the front seat were Captain Zwicky of the U.S. First Army and Lieutenant Harmon of the Florida State Police, in mufti. In the rear, Sergeant Milton Gassman slumped, his round face waxy-gray in the yellow glow of the dome light.

"Let's hear that one more time, Gassman," Zwicky said crisply. He spoke loudly, over the drum of the rain. "You and Bogen were manning your posts, a car with two unarmed civilians drives up, and then—what?"

"The guy tricked me, like I said, Cap'n. He talks nice, he looks harmless—"

"You're sure about the face?" Harmon cut in. "No scars? None at all?"

"I'm sure. I tell you, the guy was baby-faced, not even sunburned—"

"But his hair was gray?"

"Yeah, gray. I thought at first he was blond, but I seen him good in the light. But he's no old duffer. He had a wallop like a mule." Gassman rubbed his ribs gently.

"That's our boy," Harmon said. "I don't know how he covers so much ground so fast, but it's him, all right. We'll get him now. He can't be far from here in twenty minutes. A copter—"

"It's not so easy," Zwicky said. "He took off cross-country, and in this weather no copter is flying."

"Where he can go, we can follow him! He took your half-track; O.K.; so we follow him in a half-track—"

"Sure—I'll have one here in another ten minutes. That gives your man a half-hour start. If he knows how to handle a track—and I've got a hunch he does—he'll hold that lead. And up where he's headed, there are plenty of places to get lost. He'll ditch the track and—"

"You saying he's too much for the U.S. Army?"

"I'm just saying hold your horses, Mr. Harmon. I had a phone call that told me to take you along, but it didn't say anything about turning command of the company over to you. I have men and equipment to think of, in addition to a little chore of convoy escort the colonel kind of hoped I'd see to."

"Sure, sure, I'm not trying to tell you your business. But it gravels me to have to sit here and let the cop-killing son of a bitch slip through my fingers!"

"When did he kill a cop? My information was the guy broke out of jail, that's all."

"O.K., you want to get technical, he just roughed up a few cops, maybe they'll live, it's all the same to this boy."

Captain Zwicky looked hard at Harmon. "You take your job pretty personally, don't you?"

"You might say I got a personal stake in this deal."

"Just remember you're a long way out of your jurisdiction. And this is army business."

"Yeah, sure. I won't get in your way, Zwicky."

"Better make that 'Captain Zwicky' as long as you're attached to my command, Harmon."

Harmon smiled sardonically, sketched a two-finger salute—

"We don't play games with the military courtesies in this outfit, Harmon," the captain snapped. Harmon's heavy face blanked, tried a grin, then a frown. He sat up in the seat, yanked his lapels straight.

"O.K., excuse me, for Chrissake. I'm not pushing. I'm just along for the ride."

"That's right. I advise you to remember it."

In a heavy silence, they waited for the arrival of the half-track.

2

Twelve miles to the north-northwest, Colonel Ajax Pyler of the Third Armored Division, First Army, stood with a trio of regimental staff officers in the scant shelter of a big pine tree on the long slope of ground rising toward the blazing lights of the power station half a mile distant. On the road, the convoy, with dimmed headlights, stretched for five hundred yards back into the darkness. Cold rain drove at the colonel's face, blurred the lenses of the binoculars he held trained on the power station.

"Everything looks normal, Cal," he said, handing the glasses to a burly major beside him.

"I still don't get it, Colonel," the major said. "Sending a regiment of armor in here . . . what are we supposed to do, guard the place? Take a look and go home? Jesus!" He wiped rainwater from his forehead with a finger and shook his head. "Sometimes I think they're all nuts up topside."

"I'm in the dark too, Cal. My orders were to position the regiment and stand by, that's all."

"Call this a position?" The major waved at the line of vehicles.

"As far as I know, we aren't expected to attack," the colonel said with a bleak smile. He clapped the shorter man on the back. "Cheer up, Cal. We all needed the exercise—"

"Sir!" the communication tech sergeant was at the colonel's side with a field telephone. "Division on the line."

"Colonel Pyler," the officer said, turning his back to the pelting rain. He listened, frowning.

"Yes, yes. . . . I understand. About ten minutes, I'd say." He looked toward the lights of the power station as he handed the instrument back to the comm man.

"All right, gentlemen," he addressed the officers standing by. "Position your units around the periphery of a half-mile circle centered on the station—guns pointing in. Cal—detach six men under a company officer, have them stand by to escort a party of civilians in." He made a motion of dismissal as several officers started to speak at once. "That's it, gentlemen. Move out." Accompanied by the sergeant, Pyler walked back to the road, went along the line of looming light and medium tanks to the weapons carrier where his driver waited. At his instruction, the driver turned, drove back to the rear of the column. Three men in civilian clothes and raincoats stepped out of an olive-drab staff car and came over.

"All right, Mr. Crick, gentlemen, we're to proceed." The civilians, two of whom carried heavy canvas equipment kits, climbed into the high-wheeled vehicle. It turned, rolled back up past the column. At the head of the line, two jeeps waited, each carrying four men. They fell in behind. In silence the three cars proceeded along the road, following a gentle curve up the gradual slope. Ahead, a gate flanked by massive brick walls blocked the way.

While the headlights dazzled on the steel panels, two men stepped down and went forward. There was a telephone box mounted on the wall. One of the men, a lieutenant with a slung carbine, spoke into the phone. Almost at once the gates slid back. The men reentered the jeep and the three-vehicle convoy rolled ahead.

The road led straight up a number-three grade to the

high, blank walls of the power plant and the towering, light-spangled antenna farm spreading up the hillside behind it. A number of men were standing before the lighted entry to the big building. Pyler halted the ton-and-a-half and climbed down.

"Thank God you're here, Colonel," the first of the men on foot blurted as he came up. "It's been a nightmare ever since the explosion, phones out, automatic systems out, instruments out—"

"Hold on, sir," the colonel cut him off. "Better take it from the beginning—and let's get my technical people in on this." He waited until the three civilians had gathered around. By then three more men had arrived from the plant. The rain swirled and churned around them; in the glare of headlights, a million tiny crystalline tulips sprouted on the glistening pavement.

"I'm Prescott, maintenance chief," the plant man said. "Hunnicut left me in charge when he and Webb went in with explosives to blast the switch gear out of the circuit. It was all fused down, you know. Wilson went in earlier, and—but I suppose you know about that; Hunnicut reported it. Wilson died, by the way. Anyway, something went wrong, we don't know what. Hunnicut and Webb were blown to atoms—for nothing. Everything's still running full-blast—"

"You say Hunnicut is dead?" one of the civilians cut in.

"That's right. And Sam Webb, our ops chief—"

"All right, let's get down to specifics," another of the newcomers said briskly. "Give us a breakdown on exactly what's been going on here. All we've had is some garbled story that the generators won't let themselves be shut down—"

"That's not garbled, brother, that's the God's truth. And ..." The excited man went on with his account of the events of the last three hours.

The three imported experts listened in silence, with only an occasional terse question.

"... don't know what else to try," Prescott concluded. "At every point where we might have broken the circuits, the gear has fused and the surrounding areas are electrified—hot as firecrackers! We can't even get close!"

"Well?" Pyler demanded of his crew. "What about it? If Prescott's right, any ideas you may have had about walking in and throwing switches are out the window."

"I'd like to see some of this for myself," the tallest of the three civilians said. "Not that I doubt Mr. Prescott's word . . ."

"Go ahead; you'll find just what I said. But for God's sake wear protective gear!"

"Oh, I don't think that will be necessary—"

"Do as he suggests, Mr. Tadlor," Pyler ordered.

With an amused smile, Tadlor complied, donning gear from the kit he carried. His two colleagues did likewise.

"My orders are to stand by outside the building until you gentlemen give me an all-clear," Pyler growled. "Make it fast." He turned to Prescott. "How close can I bring my vehicles?"

"So far there haven't been any manifestations outside the building proper, except at the switch houses," the man said doubtfully.

Pyler gave an order; the cars pulled forward, the men walking beside them. Under the loom of the high portico, they halted. Tadlor and his aides, with Prescott, started up the steps. The doors swung abruptly open. A man staggered out, clutching himself. The sleeves of his shirt were shredded, and blood ran down his arms and dripped from his elbows. There was a scarlet blister as big as the palm of a hand along the side of his neck and jaw.

"Nagle! What happened?" Prescott rushed forward to support the man. Behind him, two more men appeared, supporting a limp female form between them.

"The whole place . . . hot . . ." Nagle crumpled. Tadlor stared at the man, went past him and up the steps, his two men behind him. Prescott called, "Colonel, don't let them —"

Tadlor's hand went out to the door. A blue spark crackled, jumped to meet him. For an instant a halo danced about the tall, lean man, then he made a comical leap into the air, fell sprawling, clownlike. His two men halted, then ran forward, bent over him. One straightened, looked down with wide eyes in a clay-pale face.

"He's dead."

"Get him back to the convoy, into a respirator!" Pyler called, motioning swiftly to the armed soldiers from the jeep.

One of the men who had helped the girl from the building turned quickly, caught Pyler's arm.

"Don't try," he croaked. "Too late."

"What do you mean?" Prescott snapped.

"You saw what happened to that fellow . . ." The man tilted his head at Tadlor's inert body.

"But—I still have forty-odd people inside—"

"Not anymore, Mr. Prescott. You left just in time. The place went crazy a few seconds after you went out. Dick and Van and I were the last to get clear. We found Jill just inside. I think she's dead. And so will anybody be who tries to go into that hellhole!"

"Into the vehicles, fast!" Pyler snapped. "Everybody!" He waited until the last man was aboard, then climbed into the weapons carrier. Behind him, Prescott leaned forward.

"Colonel—what are you going to do?"

"Tadlor's approach didn't work," he said. "So we'll try more direct methods."

"But—what . . . ?"

Pyler looked back at the man, his eyes wild in a pale,

round face. "We'll see what effect a few rounds of one-hundred-millimeter through the front door have on—on whatever it is we're fighting," he finished grimly.

3

The twin engines of the stolen half-track roared; the tracks churned futilely. The rear of the heavy vehicle sank deeper into the mud while the front wheels remained locked in the trap of broken rock that had halted the slow upward climb.

"This is as far as this bucket goes," Zabisky said. In the pale glow of the instrumental lights his round face shone with sweat. "Now what?"

Falconer unstrapped, swung open the steel door, stepped down into a soup of muck and broken rock. He scanned the horizon all around, then reached back in the vehicle to switch off the hooded driving lights. In the abrupt darkness, a faint glow was visible in the sky through the trees clothing the slope to the left.

"A little reconnaissance," Falconer said. He made his way up through brush to the ridge, looked down across the spread of dark countryside at a rectilinear arrangement of lights perhaps two miles away. Other, smaller lights ringed the central concentration in a loose circle a mile in diameter.

Zabisky arrived, puffing. "Brother, you move fast in the dark." He stared in the direction Falconer was looking.

"What's that? Looks like some kind of plant. This what we been looking for?"

"No."

"Funny place for a factory, out in the sticks fifty miles from noplace."

Light winked brilliantly below: once, twice, three times. Some of the lights of the central installation faded.

"Hey—what gives?" Zabisky grunted. A dull *carrump, carrump . . . carrump* floated up to them.

"Artillery fire," Falconer said.

"Look, pal, you ain't here to get mixed up with the army, I hope?"

"By no means."

"Maybe you better tell me what this is all about, huh? I don't want to get the U.S. infantry mad at me. I'm pretty dumb, but there's got to be a connection: you busting a gut to get to this patch of noplace just when somebody starts shooting. What are you, some kind of foreign spy? Or what?"

Falconer turned to Zabisky. "You'd better go back, John. I'm going on from here on foot—alone."

"Hey, wait a minute," Zabisky protested. "Just like that, you're going to walk off into the woods and—"

"That's right, John. You can make it back to the road by dawn."

"Have a heart, mister," Zabisky protested. "I come this far. What's all this? What's the shooting? Why—"

"Good-bye, John." Falconer turned and started upslope, following a faint footpath, angling away from the lights below. Zabisky called after him, but he ignored his shouts.

4

"You're a fool if you think I'm going to help you, Max," Hardman said.

"Don't call me 'Max'; we're not on that kind of terms." The prisoner smiled a gaunt smile. He was sitting at ease in the big leather chair beside Hardman's desk, puffing one of Hardman's cigarettes. The muzzle of the big-caliber solid-slug pistol rested on the desk, aimed at Hardman's chest. "It's 'Mr. Wiston'—or just 'Wiston.' And you'll do like I say, Warden." He had a deep, gravelly voice, soft but penetrating.

Hardman shook his head. "I couldn't get you out of the prison even if I wanted to, Max," he said easily. "And I don't want to."

"Warden, you think I wouldn't shoot you as soon as look at you?" Wiston's voice was mild, his tone curious.

"Sure, you'd shoot me if you thought it would buy you your freedom. But you know it would all be over for you if you shot me in cold blood. I'm your one chance to get clear—you think. But you're wrong—"

"For God's sake, Governor," Lester Pale whispered from the chair against the wall where Wiston had ordered him to sit. "You convince him of that and he'll kill you out of hand!"

"No he won't," Hardman said. "He knows I'm the only one who can help him—if not to escape, at least to bail him out of some of the trouble he's gotten himself into tonight."

"Warden, you talk too much," Wiston said. "I'll tell you just how it is: I've waited ten years for this chance, I'm riding it all the way. Maybe it's true what you say about all the fancy safety gadgets and automatic traps and that— but I'd rather be dead than stay in this box any longer. We're walking out of here, me and you—win, lose, or draw. So maybe you better do what you can to get those gates open. Cause I'm not going back in that cellblock alive, ever. And if I have to die, I'm taking you along, I promise you that, Warden."

"He means it, Governor," Pale said.

"The pansy's right," Wiston said, smiling. "Now, let's get moving. I'm getting restless. I want to smell that fresh air, Warden, see that open sky, feel that rain on my face." He stood abruptly, motioning with the gun. Hardman didn't move. Wiston swung the gun to one side and without looking fired a round into the wall two feet from Lester Pale's chair.

"Next one hits meat, Warden."

Hardman stood.

"This won't work, Max," he said. "It's hopeless."

"Sure. Let's go."

In the corridor, sounds of distant shouting were audible.

"I set 'em to raising hell down in the services wing," Wiston said. "That'll keep your screws tied up whilst you and me try the back way."

"What back way?"

"The water gate, Warden. That was always the weak spot here at Caine. Could never dope the tunnel, though. But you'll get me through. You'll say all the right things and get me through."

"Then what? The road only leads to Gull Key—"

"There's a lot of water out there, Warden. I'm a strong swimmer. And I know these waters. I fished amongst these islands for many a year before ever they built the prison. Don't worry about me, Warden. I'll be fine, just fine."

"In this storm you'll drown before you've swum a hundred yards."

"Don't talk, Warden. Just lead the way."

In silence, Hardman pushed through the stairwell door. In darkness, he descended, feeling his way; Wiston's footsteps followed directly behind him. At the bottom, he felt over the wall, found the door that opened into the Proccessing Room.

"There may be some of my men in here," he said. "I hope you have sense enough not to start shooting, Max."

"We'll see."

Hardman opened the door; it swung in on darkness.

"Now what?" he said. "Neither of us can see—"

Wiston's fingers touched him, hooked his belt. "You know the layout, Warden. Just keep going. When I'm unhappy, you'll hear this gun go off. Or will you? You know what they say about the one that kills you."

Hardman tried to remember the layout of the room. The personnel doors were to the right . . . about there. He moved forward cautiously, the other man at his heels. His hands touched brickwork. He explored, found the cold steel of the door. It swung open at his touch. Chill air moved around his face. The sounds of the storm were louder now.

"Good work, Warden. I can smell the Gulf."

"This is the garage," Hardman said. "The only exit is through the big doors. They're power-operated. This is the end of the line, Max—"

A beam of light speared out from the left. Hardman whirled, shouted, "Douse that, you damn fool!"

The boom of the gun racketed and echoed in the enclosed space. The flashlight dropped to the floor and rolled, throwing its beam across the oil-stained concrete floor. There was a heavy, complicated sound of a body falling against the side of a vehicle, sliding down to the floor, a gargly rattle of exhaled air.

"Don't move, Warden," Wiston said calmly. "I'm going to pick up the light."

Hardman heard soft, quick steps. The light swung up, flicked across him, on across to the spot where a man in coveralls lay on his face between two armored personnel carriers in a widening pool of black-red blood.

"Too bad," Wiston said. "I didn't mean that feller no harm, but he shouldn't of put the light on me thataway." He shone the light on the big garage doors, up one side, across the top, down the other.

"O.K., your time, Warden. Get 'em open."

"I told you—"

"Reckon there's a manual rig someplace. Better find it."

"Find it yourself, Wiston."

"You're a funny one, Warden. You saw me, just now;

you know I'm not bashful about using the gun. You figure you're bulletproof?"

"I'm here to keep cold-blooded killers like you out of circulation, Wiston, not to lead you outside and wave bye-bye."

Wiston laughed. "You're a harder nut than you look, old man. But I wonder, are you as hard as you talk?" The convict held the flashlight beam on Hardman's right knee. "I count five. Then I put a bullet where the light is. After that, I ask you again." He cleared his throat, spat, began to count . . .

Hardman waited until the count of four, another half-second, then pivoted, dropped toward the floor as the gun boomed. A red-hot sledgehammer struck him behind the right knee, flipped him. His face hit hard, skidding on the concrete. There seemed to be a spike driven into the back of his leg. He tried to draw a breath to yell, tried to get his hand on the spike to pull it out—

"Stop flopping, Warden. I should of killed you for that trick, but you're just winged."

The light was dazzling in Hardman's eyes, growing and receding. Blood pounded in his head. Sickness swelled inside him. Pain rolled out in white-hot waves from his shattered knee. He hardly heard Wiston's voice. He lay on his side, his cheek against the floor, clutching his leg.

"Now, you better just tell me about that door, Warden. . . ." The man was standing over him; he saw the dusty, dark-blue legs of the prison trousers, the sturdy shoes, through a veil of agony.

"Go . . . hell . . ." he managed.

The feet went away. There were sounds, thumping, the rattle of metal, curses. Then a grunt of satisfaction; a steady ratcheting noise started up, accompanied by heavy breathing. Cold wet air was sweeping in across the floor; the shrill of wind and the drumming of rain were abruptly louder. The ratcheting ceased.

Hardman tried to roll over on his back, succeeded in banging his head against the floor. He forced his hands, slippery with blood, away from his wound, pushed himself to a sitting position. The man Wiston had shot lay ten feet from him, visible by the light of the flash which Wiston had placed on the floor. The garage door had been raised a foot and a half. Wiston had picked up the light, was sliding under the door. He cleared it, got to his feet, moving away.

Abruptly, bright, hard flashes of light winked, the stutter of automatic weapons racketed in the drive well, casting shadows that moved like silent-movie actors. Lying on the floor just inside the door, Hardman saw a man walking toward him. The man slowed, knelt slowly, fell forward on his face. Other men were coming; bright lights glared, reflecting from wet pavement. Voices called out. Wiston lay on his face a yard from Hardman. His hands groped over the pavement. He lifted his head and looked into Hardman's eyes.

"Someplace," he said. "Sometime, there's got . . . got to be . . . be . . . some justice. . . ." His face hit the pavement.

A foot turned Wiston over. The rain fell on his wide-open eyes.

"Did you get that?" someone said. "He goes out talking about justice. A punk like that."

There was something that Hardman wanted to say then, something of vast importance that he had tried all his life to understand and that now, in this instant, was clear to him. But when he opened his mouth, darkness filled his brain and swept him away into a black maelstrom of roaring waters.

5

Private Obers, Ewen J., ASN 3783746353, of the Third Company, First Battalion, paused in the lee of one of the big trees to wipe the icy rainwater from his face and try one more time to adjust the collar of the G.I. raincoat to prevent the cold trickle down the back of his neck. He propped his M-3 carbine against the tree, undid the top button with cold-numbed fingers, turned up the collar of the field jacket under the coat, rebuttoned the coat. It felt colder and clammier than ever, but it was the best he could do. He considered pulling off his boots to empty the water from them; but what the hell; they'd just fill up again. Every third step was into a gully with water anywhere from ankle- to knee-deep. Obers peered through the darkness for signs of the platoon. Pitcher had told them to keep it closed up while they worked their way upslope from the road where they'd left the six-by's. He hadn't seen Dodge or Shapiro, the men on his left and right, since they'd hit the rough ground. But at least you couldn't get lost; not if you just kept climbing.

Obers wished briefly that he were back in the barracks, racked out on his bunk, reading a magazine and eating a candy bar; then he slung the carbine and stepped out to face the rain anew.

There was a movement above him.

"Shapiro?" His call was muffled by the storm.

There was no answer; but above, a dark shape moved, low to the ground, big—too big to be Shapiro—or Dodge; and why was the guy crawling? Obers halted, feeling a sudden prickling at the back of his neck—not that he believed in spooks. . . .

"All right, who's there?" he yelled against the rain.

No answer. The big shape—well over six feet long— flowed downward toward him. For an instant, Obers thought he caught a gleam of light reflected from yellow-green eyes. He swung the carbine around, jacked the loading lever, aimed it from the hip, and pulled the trigger.

Nothing happened; the trigger was locked hard. Panic flooded up in Obers. *Safety's on!* The words popped into his mind; but his finger was locked on the trigger, squeezing until the metal cut into his flesh. And the dark shape was rising, flowing outward and down toward him.

In the last split second, he tried to scream, but there was no breath in his lungs. Then the weight struck him, threw him down and back. He felt something icy cold rake across his throat, felt a remote pain that was hardly noticeable in the greater agony of the need for air. Something scarlet red dazzled before his eyes, grew until it was a sunburst that filled the world, then slowly faded into an endless darkness.

In a clearing in the forest stands a tall man with a mane of flame-red hair, dressed in garments of green leather and a surcoat of buff ornamented with a white bird with spread wings. A two-handed sword with a jeweled pommel hangs at his side. A bow is slung at his back. He wears a heavy gauntlet on his left hand, on which is perched a white hawk, from whose head the man has just removed a hood of soft leather. With a lift of his wrist, the man tosses the bird high; it gives a piercing cry and circles high into the air.

"My lord's power over a wild bird is a thing to wonder at," murmurs one of a huddle of serfs watching from concealment.

"Indeed, 'tis a matter passing Christian understanding," another comments.

"I've heard it said," says another, "that the bird is a were-creature, a man enchanted."

"Aye, 'tis his own brother, some say—"

"Nay, not his brother; him he slew in battle before the eyes of all his men—"

"But by the virtue of Christ, the slain brother rose and walked again—"

"—and 'twas then he enchanted him into the form of the white falcon—"

"Old wives' tales," says the first man who spoke, a dark

163

man with strange yellow eyes. "My Lord Lohengrin is no magician, but a true knecht—"

"Bah! What do you know?" speaks up an oldster with a straggly yellow beard. "I served him in your granfer's time, and with my own eyes oft have I seen him quaff deep of the waters of eternal youth. For does he not—aye, and the bird as well—appear today as he did then, when I was a lusty stripling—"

"You lusty, Brecht? When was that, before or after the Flood of Noah?"

When the furtive laughter dies, a man who has not spoken tugs at his ear portentously. "Aye, laugh," he says. "But in truth you are all wide of the mark. The bird is no man ensorceled."

The others look at him with slack jaws.

"'Tis a woman, Leda by name, a humble maid who spurned my Lord's base advances. This I know, for gospel fact, because she was the sister of a cousin of a close friend—"

"Bah!" scoffs the elder. "If 'twere a woman, she would take the shape of a swan, not a hunting falcon; any fool knows that—"

"So you do," the other says sharply. "But a wise man knows better—"

They fall silent as the hunter turns and looks across at them with cold blue eyes that penetrate to their hiding place.

"You are all wide of the mark," he says in a voice like the ring of cold iron. "The bird is only a bird; my brother is a mad dog; and as for myself—I am a dead man."

As one, the gaggle of villagers whirl and pelt away through the underbrush. The falconer smiles a lean smile, stands looking up at the sky where the white bird circles on a rising current of air.

Chapter Eleven

1

Grayle had covered twelve miles in less than an hour, running steadily across the dark, rain-swept fields, ignoring the pain from his side. Now, in the broken ground below the high rampart of the hills, he found his progress slowed. It was necessary to pick his way, splashing through rushing torrents of muddy water flowing down over the barrier of boulders deposited ten thousand years ago by the glacier. Once he paused, listening to the sound of what seemed to be heavy gunfire in the distance, but the sound was not repeated. Minutes later he became aware of men moving on the slope ahead and to his left. The ground was steep here, a rubble-heap of rock fallen from the steep cliffs above; the men were noisy, calling to each other, occasionally flashing hand-lights across the slope, through the scrub pines that had found a foothold here. It was apparent that they were soldiers: a sergeant barked angry orders for silence to the members of the Third Platoon.

Grayle skirted the men, who were working their way southward, to his left, and continued his climb, facing into the driving rain.

He was close now. It would not be much longer before he knew if he had been in time.

2

Outside, the unceasing storm buffeted the thick walls; inside, the generator chugged, the stink of exhaust fumes hung in the stale air. Hardman lay on a field cot set up in his office, his right leg heavily bandaged.

"You look bad, Governor," Brasher said, frowning. "You ought to be—"

"Skip all that. Let's have that report."

"Well—if you think you're competent—that is, feeling well enough—"

"The report, Brasher." Hardman's voice was tight with pain. "You like to deliver reports, remember? It gives you a chance to sound like Moses—or is it God in person?"

"Look here—" Brasher started angrily.

"That's an order, Captain!" Hardman's snarl overrode the other. Brasher's face twitched angrily. "I was thinking of your welfare, Governor. However, as you insist," he hurried on, "you know about the car theft and assault in Brooksville. Well, that was just a warm-up, it seems. Our man proceeded to Gainesville, attacked two patrolmen and stole their car, drove it to the downtown police-helicopter facility, and proceeded to hijack a high-speed military recon machine—"

"Who told you this cock-and-bull story?" Hardman cut in.

"Captain Lacey. And—"

"All right, he drove in to the middle of a heavily manned police installation, borrowed a copter, and took off in a hurricane. Anything else?"

"The copter was followed on radar; it headed north-west. The plot was passed to Eglin, and on to other bases along the route. They tracked him to within a hundred miles of the Canadian border. Then someone—Washington, I think—scrambled fighters out of Great

Lakes. They forced him down in rough country in northern Minnesota."

"You're serious about this?"

"Dead serious."

"And—where is he now?"

"He got clear. But they got the girl."

"What girl?"

"His accomplice. The one who helped him escape."

"What has she told them?"

Brasher shook his head. "I understand she was pretty badly shaken up in the crash. She hasn't talked."

"You said he got clear. Weren't they covering the ground?"

"Certainly—but that's a big country—"

"He's alone and unarmed, probably injured. He should be easy enough to take."

"Well, as to that—I should point out that there *are* a couple of confusing points. It seems there's a report of a man answering Grayle's description attacking two police officers at the scene of an auto accident."

"Near the crash scene?"

"About seventy miles southwest."

"How does the time tie in?"

"The crash occurred at four-oh-seven; this other item was about an hour later, five-oh-one A.M."

"So now he's in two places at once," Hardman snorted. "What makes you think there's any connection? There are thousands of men who answer Grayle's general description."

"Not that can tear the door off a car," Brasher said, looking sideways at Hardman.

"What does that mean?"

"The FBI looked the car over—the one that was wrecked. It was one of theirs. It was tailing Grayle. The door was ripped from its hinges. And there were finger-marks in the metal."

Hardman was propped on one elbow. "And?" he prompted.

"He assaulted the police, as I said, and left the scene in his car. Twenty miles up the road, he and his accomplice—"

"A girl?"

"No, a man. They hit an army roadblock, attacked a couple of soldiers, and stole a military vehicle—a half-track, I think it was."

"All this, less than an hour after he crashed a stolen police copter in another place, accompanied by a woman. Quite a trick, eh, Brasher? A real superman, this fellow—either that, or the police forces of this country are a collection of idiots!"

"I know it sounds crazy." Brasher waved his hands. "But these are the facts reported to me! This man gets around faster than a dirty rumor! It has to be Grayle! Sure, anybody could have gray hair and a red stubble, but who else could tear steel with his bare hands? Unless . . ." Brasher looked startled. "A minute ago you said something about a superman, Governor," he said. "What would you say to *two* supermen?"

"I don't know, Brasher." Hardman lay back, looking exhausted.

"Well, I'll be getting along, Governor." Brasher glanced at the big gold strap-watch on his wrist. "Things are breaking fast; there'll no doubt be an arrest at any moment—"

"Brasher," Hardman called as the policeman turned away.

"When they catch him—either or both of him—I want him taken alive."

Brasher looked grave. "Well, now, Governor, as we agreed earlier, we don't want to place any obstacles in the path of law enforcement—"

"I said alive, Brasher!"

"What if this mad dog begins shooting down more police officers? What are they supposed to do? Turn the other cheek?"

"Alive, Brasher," Hardman repeated. "Now, get out—and maybe you'd better tell that doctor to call the hospital after all."

Outside, Lester Pale was waiting. He raised his eyebrows.

"Nothing," Brasher said quickly. "He was conscious—just barely. He didn't say anything that made sense."

"No change in the orders? I had the idea—"

"No change," Brasher snapped. "I'm a cop, remember? My job is to catch crooks, that's all."

3

Halfway up the hill where he had abandoned the half-track, Falconer lay flat on wet ground among dense-growing brush. From the darkness ahead and to the left came the sounds of a man forcing his way through the growth. Other sounds of passage came from the right, along with the occasional gleam of a flashlight. Gradually, the sounds receded as the men passed by, moving diagonally to his course. Falconer rose, gained another fifty feet, then paused, head up, sniffing the air. Cautiously he advanced, skirting a giant tree. The sharp, metallic odor he had noticed grew rapidly stronger. Then he saw the body.

It was a soldier, sprawled at the base of the big pine, hands outflung, one leg doubled under him. The front of the man's raincoat was shredded; pale skin slashed by deep cuts showed through the rents. Above, the throat was gashed from ear to ear, not once, but in three parallel wounds. The ground under the man was a gluey soup of blood and muck.

For half a minute Falconer studied the corpse and the ground around it through narrowed eyes. Then he went on.

4

Tech Sergeant Duane Pitcher of the Third Platoon was disgusted. For the past hour, ever since they'd left the vehicles on the road below, he'd been stumbling around half-frozen in the pouring rain in these damned pitch-black woods, trying to follow orders to make no noise and show no lights, and to keep the men spread out in some kind of skirmish line, and keep 'em moving up toward the position the lieutenant had shown him on the contour map. In this soup, he'd be lucky to get within a mile of it. It was bad enough just to climb these damned slippery rocks through this damned slippery mud, but he had to be in twenty places at once, because otherwise the eager beavers like Obers would be a hundred yards out in front, and goldbricks like Bloom and Ginty would flake out and wind up back at the trucks, claiming they got lost.

Pitcher saw a dim movement ahead, called, got an answer in a Deep South rumble.

"O.K., hold it up here, Brown. We don't want to run into the Second Platoon coming down."

He moved on obliquely across the slope, made contact with two more men.

"Where's Obers?" he asked a two-striper.

"Hell, Sarge, where's anybody in this stuff?"

Pitcher grunted. "O.K., hold the platoon where they're at. Lieutenant Boyd's supposed to make contact on the left before we top the ridge. I got to look for Obers before he walks down and gets a one-hundred-millimeter in his lap."

"What was the firing, Sarge?"

"How do I know?" Pitcher moved up along a faint path through the trees. He had covered seventy yards when he tripped over an obstruction at the base of a big pine. Pitcher's training was good. As he stumbled, he swung the carbine from his shoulder, hit the ground and rolled, came to rest in firing position, gun aimed, safety off.

Nothing moved. There was no sound but the howl of the wind, the crash of rain. He hadn't liked the feel of what he had stepped on. It was too soft, too yielding. It felt like . . .

He unclipped the flash at his belt, flicked it in the direction of the tree. It shone on a booted foot. The rest of the man was there too, lying on his back. It was Obers. Pitcher held the light on the torn throat, the lacerated chest.

For a long moment he held the light on the dead man. Then he shifted the beam, shone it around him into the high darkness of the forest. There was nothing but wet trees, wet rock. Then a sound came from his left below: the snap of a sodden twig, the slither of shoes in mud, the scrape of leather against rock. Pitcher switched off the light, dropped it, fitted the stock of the carbine against his cheek, his finger on the trigger.

A man appeared, toiling upward through the trees. He was a big fellow, dressed in a waterproof mackinaw. Wet black hair was plastered to his round skull. He was headed straight for the spot where the body lay. Pitcher put the light square in his eyes.

"All right, hold it right there!" Pitcher called. At the words, the man froze, then whirled, jumped for the underbrush. Pitcher's finger jerked; red flame gouted. The shot was a flat *bam!* against the background of the storm. The man stumbled, caught himself, plunged on into the brush. Pitcher fired again into the darkness where he had disappeared, but when he came forward to investigate, there was only a footprint and a splash of fast-dissolving blood to show that there had been a target and that his bullets had found it.

5

Falconer had halted when he heard the shots, then, hearing nothing more, resumed his climb. The trail ended on a bare slope of stone across which water sluiced like a spillway. He crossed it, hugging the rock, while the wind drove rain into his eyes and nose, under his clothes. At the upper edge, giant rocks lay tumbled like debris from some titanic explosion. Falconer picked his way up through them, and was looking down into a hollow, pooled with darkness like ink. He took a step forward, and abruptly there was no rain; the buffeting wind was gone. A foot away, the storm still shrieked, but here the air was still and warm. There was a soft sound from below; a vertical line of yellow light appeared and widened, shining out on dry rock, reflecting on a sleek curve of age-blackened metal. Beyond the open doorway gleamed pale-green walls, polished brightwork.

"Welcome, Commander Lokrien," a mellow voice rang out in a strange language that for a moment Falconer almost failed to comprehend. "I have waited long for this hour."

6

Standing in the road beside the medium tank which, half an hour before, had fired three rounds of conventional 100 mm. through the main entrance to the Upper Pasmaquoddie Power Station, Colonel Ajax Pyler propped his fists on his hips and thrust his face closer to that of the divisional staff observer.

"You don't know the situation, Yount!" he snapped. "I

saw it kill a man right in front of me! I talked to the three men that managed to get clear! I'm telling you this is more than a malfunction or a damn fool plot by a crazy engineer!"

"There are some forty civilian personnel still inside that building, Pyler," Colonel Yount came back coolly. "We have only the word of a couple of half-hysterical civilians that there's anything wrong in there that a platoon of foot soldiers can't control—"

"I'm not sending a man of my command into that death trap," Pyler said flatly. "I don't give a damn if the commanding general personally wrote out the order in his own blood with a bent pin!"

"Pyler, you're trigger-happy—"

"My orders were to shut down that transmitter. I intend to do just that—any way I can!"

"That's a five-billion-dollar federal installation you're shelling, man! This isn't Vietnam! You can't just blow anything that gets in your way to kingdom come!"

"I can try!"

"Before you do," Yount said coldly, "I suggest you think for a few moments about trying less drastic measures than total destruction of the plant."

"Who said anything about total destruction? I intend to place rounds in carefully selected spots, as pointed out by my engineers, until transmission ceases. Then—"

"No you're not, Pyler." Yount made a swift motion, and the big master sergeant who had been standing by at parade rest staring straight out under the rim of his steel helmet came to life.

"Sir!"

"Colonel Pyler, this is Sergeant Major Muldoon. He weighs two hundred and forty pounds, stripped, and there's not an ounce of fat on him. I've ordered him to escort you back to divisional HQ to make your report. . . ."

Pyler's face went pale, then purpled.

"That is, unless you're willing to listen to reason."

Pyler drew a couple of hoarse breaths through his nose.

"What . . . what do you have in mind?"

"I want to send a three-man team into the plant. Specially equipped, of course; I'm not completely discounting your description of conditions inside. It seems there are several points at which the circuitry can be interrupted quite simply—"

"I told you what happened to that engineer fellow, Hunnicut, and the other man—and before them there was another—"

"I know all about that. I've talked to Prescott. My men know what to do."

"Very well," Pyler said through stiff lips. "I'll want written orders relieving me, of course."

Yount shook his head. "You're not relieved, Jack. I'm just lending what you might call a little tech support from headquarters." He turned away, began giving instructions to a tall, blond-haired captain and two noncoms, all in black commando assault dress.

7

Lieutenant Harmon of the Florida State Police was the first to spy the abandoned half-track blocking the gullied trail above. He and Captain Zwicky climbed down from their machine, slogged forward, guns in hand.

"Well, what did you expect, to find your man sitting in it eating his lunch?" Zwicky asked as Harmon cursed the empty vehicle.

"The son of a bitch can't be far. Let's get him!"

Zwicky squinted up through swirling rain at the dark forest above. "You think you could find him up there?"

"Got any better ideas?"

"Maybe." Zwicky indicated the low rise to the east. "The Pasmaquoddie Power Plant's just the other side of the hill a couple of miles. Maybe that's where he was headed."

"What the hell would he want to go there for?"

"I don't know—but there's some kind of trouble over there. That's why the army's out in the weather. Maybe your man has something to do with it?"

"Like what? For Christ's sake, Captain, this bum is a con on the lam, a lousy killer who spent his life in stir. What—"

"I don't know. But this is the only inhabited spot in forty miles; this is wild country, Lieutenant. And your man headed right for it. It's worth looking into, isn't it? Or are you dead set on climbing up there to beat the bushes for him—alone? Because this is as far as I go."

Harmon looked up toward the heights above.

"Well—"

There was a sound from nearby—the unmistakable double *clack-clack!* of the arming lever of a rifle.

"Freeze right there!" a harsh voice barked from the darkness.

Harmon dropped his pistol, hoisted his hands where he stood, his back to the voice. Zwicky turned slowly, holding the carbine by the breech, muzzle down, out from his side.

A uniformed man came forward, holding a carbine leveled. There were tech sergeant's stripes painted on the helmet that concealed his eyes.

"What is this, Sergeant?" Zwicky said.

"Hey!" another voice spoke up. "The guy's an officer, for Chrissakes!"

The sergeant paused, looking uncertainly from Zwicky to Harmon, who was looking back over his shoulder. The latter lowered his hands.

"G.I.'s!" he blurted. "For God's sake, Zwicky, tell them—"

"Get 'em up—high!" the noncom snapped. "You, too, Cap'n."

"Maybe you'd better tell me just what the hell you think you're doing," Zwicky said, not moving.

"Maybe you'd better drop it, Cap'n, before I pull this trigger. I've lost one man tonight, and I'm not messing around."

Zwicky let the gun fall. "All right, tell it, soldier."

"You better tell me what you're doing in my platoon area, Cap'n. And who's this fellow?" He jerked his head at Harmon.

"He's a police officer. We're looking for the man who drove the track up here." Zwicky motioned with his head toward the big vehicle behind him.

"Gus, take a look at their ID's. Don't get between me and them."

A corporal came forward, slung his carbine, grinned sheepishly as he patted Zwicky's pockets, brought out his wallet, opened it, and showed the blue card to the sergeant, who studied it by the light of the flash another man held. The corporal took Harmon's badge, showed it to the other.

"All right, I've played along with you, Sergeant," Zwicky said as he pocketed his wallet. "Now, aim that piece in some other direction and tell me what the hell is going on here."

The sergeant lowered the carbine reluctantly. "One o' my men's dead up there. Obers, worth any other three men in the outfit. I'm looking for the man that did it." He glanced at the track. "Maybe—"

"Sure it's him!" Harmon burst out. "The man's a cold-blooded killer, an escaped convict!" He looked at Zwicky. "I told you about this boy, Captain. Now maybe you'll listen to me!"

"Let's take a look," Zwicky said. He picked up his carbine, wiped mud from it on his sleeve. Harmon scooped up his pistol.

"Gus, you take the point," the sergeant ordered the corporal. "Cap'n, you and the civilian next. I'll be right behind."

It took the group of men a quarter of an hour to pick their way upslope to the spot where Obers' body lay. Harmon whistled as he stared down at the mutilated corpse.

"O.K.," he said. "Now you see what kind of guy we're working with. Kid gloves, hah? Like hell, Captain; like hell."

"There's some kind of trail leading up here," one of the men said. "Hey!" He pointed excitedly to a sheltered spot under a clump of foliage. "Footprints—a couple of 'em!"

"Sure, I seen the bastard," the sergeant said. "I winged him, but he got clear. When I heard noises down below, I figured maybe he'd doubled back."

Harmon grunted. "He's up there," he said. "And I say let's get him."

The sergeant looked at Harmon. "You're a cop," he said. "If I go up there, I aim to shoot first and chin with the son of a bitch later."

"Can't say I blame you," Harmon said.

"Gus, you take the detail," the sergeant said. "I'll be back when I've cleared my barrel into somebody's gut."

With Zwicky in the lead, the three men started up the final ascent.

It is dusk; against the dust-red sky, the flashes of the besieging cannon wink ceaselessly across the folds of the hills below the walls of the town. From the gates, a party of five men ride out on war horses, gaunt black steeds whose ribs stand out like the cheekbones of their helmeted and corseleted riders, one of whom carries a couched lance from the tip of which a white pennon flutters. Four of the men are olive-dark, black-bearded. One is smooth-shaven, with black-red hair and a scarred face. He sits a head taller in the saddle than any of his companions and rides before them.

Another party of five men sit their horses on the brow of the slope. These men are better fed; one has black hair and a cat's eyes. One, with hair the color of new rust, sits in advance of the others, dressed in rich but well-worn war gear, a sword at his side, a shield slung at his saddle bow.

The oncoming party halts fifty feet distant. The leader speaks briefly to his men, swings down from his mount, comes forward. The rust-haired man dismounts, advances to meet him. They are of a height, one wider, thicker of wrist and neck, the other quicker-moving, lighter-footed.

"I knew it was you," the big-boned man says. "I saw your cursed fowl coursing above the field."

"Yet you came. . . ."

"Have no fear: I honor the white ensign."

The flame-haired man laughs softly.

"Many loyal men starve in the town," the bigger man says. *"This charade must end."*

"Then cease your harassment of my merchants—"

"Let them peddle their wares at home! These people have no need of better steel and improved gunpowder; they do slaughter enough with their own crude means."

"I regret the uses to which knowledge is put, but that is the price of a growing technology."

"The price is too high; these barbarians are not ready—"

"I've told you my terms, de la Torre—as I believe you style yourself these days."

"Because of those who trust me, I must yield. But we will meet again, brother."

"No doubt, brother."

They turn; each rejoins his own men. De la Torre's chief lieutenant eyes the flame-haired man as he mounts his white horse.

"My lord, why not kill him now—a swift shaft in the back—"

His master catches him by the arm, lifts him to his toes.

"He is mine, Castillo—mine and no other's!"

Across the hill, the cat-eyed man rides close beside his lord.

"Surely it would have been wise to dispatch the traitor on the spot," he is saying. *"A single prick of a poisoned dart—"*

"No."

"But, lord—doubtless he plots new betrayal—"

"You lie, Pinquelle!"

"I sometimes wonder, lord, whether truly it be hate—or love—that you feel for him."

The master reins in, wheels to face his lackey. *"Get thee*

gone from my company, Pinquelle! I tire of thy pinched face and thy cruel eyes and thy poisonous tongue."

"As my lord wishes." The man turns his mount and rides away, not looking back.

Chapter Twelve

1

Captain Aldous Drake, Special Forces, on detached duty with HQ, Third Army, lay flat on his belly in sodden grass a hundred and thirty feet from the fire-blackened orifice that had been the glass-and-aluminum main entrance to the power plant. A typist's chair lay on its side among the rubble half-blocking the entry. A strip of tattered scarlet carpet was draped over the littered porch and down the steps like the tongue of a dead animal. Smoke still drifted from the blackened interior of the entry hall.

"Pyler messed up the front door pretty bad," Staff Sergeant Ike Weintraub said, hugging the ground a few feet to Drake's left.

"That's O.K. We don't plan to waltz in there anyway. Ike, there's your spot, off to the left, past the bushes." Drake indicated a vertical ventilator slot cutting the featureless concrete front. "A few ounces of PMM ought to open a hole wide enough to slide in through. Jess ..." He addressed the big black-faced three-striper on his right. "Think you can get up on the roof—over there, to the right, above the terrace?"

"Sure, no sweat."

"When you get up there, keep low, look for the freight-elevator shaft. You know how to jimmy it." Drake looked at his watch.

"I make it five minutes and thirty seconds after." He

waited while the other two made minute adjustments to their timepieces. "Ike, I'm giving you five minutes to set your charges. Jess, you have your spot picked. Use your power jimmy, but no blasting. I may break a little glass getting in. We'll spread out inside—you know the layout from the maps—and each go for his own target. First man to score sets off a screamer, and we get the hell out. All right, let's go."

"Cap'n—when we break away—will it be a category three, or what?"

"Category one, Ike. Every man for himself. Our reports may make all the difference to the next team. But I'm betting both you bums a fifth of the good stuff we all make it clean. Let's go." Drake slid forward, using his elbows and toes in a quick, comical rhythm that ate up the distance with deceptive swiftness and in total silence. For a few seconds he could see his two compatriots as dark blurs against darkness; then they were gone.

Ahead the building waited, high, bright-lit, crossed by slanting lines of rain. Fifty feet from the facade, Drake encountered bits of debris: glass, brick fragments, a scrap of upholstery material, papers. He crossed a sidewalk, another strip of grass, eased under a line of low-growing juniper, and was against the face of the building.

The windows—fixed double panels of heavy plastic— were just above him, the sills at face level, the room behind them dark. Drake came to his feet to the left of the opening, opened a pouch clipped to his pistol belt, took out a lump of a dark-green material resembling modeling clay. He formed it swiftly into a long, slender tube, packed it along the edge of the windows, working two feet out from the corner along the bottom and side. He inserted a tiny glass-encased capsule in the corner, attached a pair of hair-fine wires, and withdrew along the face of the building a distance of ten feet. He went flat, face down, and brought his wristwatch up under his eyes. Three and a half minutes elapsed; ninety seconds to go.

The rain pounded Drake's back. The cold mud under his chest soaked through his combat jacket, found chinks in his weather suit. He flexed his hands to keep them limber. Never tell what you might run into inside. Yount had talked as if the whole thing was an exercise, but the other bird—Pyler, his name was—had been pretty shook up. Too bad he hadn't had a chance to talk to the men who'd come out of the plant, but Yount had passed on everything useful—or so he said. Not that it amounted to much. But for what it was worth, the pattern looked simple. The corridors were electrified, the switches, door hardware, everything you'd normally touch. So the trick was to make your own holes, stick to the service ways, go straight for the spot the tech boys had shown him on the drawings, and zap! The job was done. After all, it was just a pile of machinery in there. Pull the plug, and it had to quit; it was as easy as that.

Ten seconds to go. Drake hoped Ike was ready—and that Jess had his spot picked. If there *was* some nut inside, some mad-genius type, hitting him in three places at once ought to keep him hopping. Five seconds. Too bad if he wasn't quite close enough to the building and a pound or two of pulverized Plexiglas hit him in the back.

Drake thumbed the detonator button. There was an instantaneous ear-shattering blast, and dirt gouted beside his face. He came to his feet, slid along the wall to the now glassless opening, reached in for a grip, jumped, pulled himself up over the sill, and dropped onto a glass-littered carpet. He rolled to the wall, stopped with his feet spread, toes out, elbow braced, the pistol in his hand aimed toward the door. Dust was still settling. A piece of glass fell softly to the rug. A corpse lay face down near the desk. All right, Drake thought. Where's Ike's shot? . . .

He felt the dull blast through the floor before the sound

came; Drake let out a breath and looked around the room. The entry to the access system the engineers had pointed out was in the ceiling of the toilet opening onto the office. The door was six feet away, standing ajar. Drake stood; as he did, he noticed a pale light glowing against the rug. A corridor light shining under the door, hitting the rug fibers? No, too bright for that. More of a fluorescence—and getting brighter, rippling like the glow in hot embers. A spark leaped across the rug. Drake backed a step; his elbow touched a filing cabinet. In the next instant, blue fire enveloped him. He had time to draw one breath—a breath of flames that scorched his lungs— and to expel it in a ragged screech of agony. Then his charred body fell stiffly, lay smoking on the floor, the half-slagged pistol still gripped in his blackened finger bones.

Sixty feet distant, in the ground-floor mechanical-equipment room, Ike Weintraub paused in wrapping a field bandage around the gash he had received on his forearm from a wild fragment from his shot, his head cocked. The sound had been very faint, but it had sounded a lot like a yell—a scream, to be exact. But it was probably just wind, whistling around some of the holes they'd knocked in the walls. Felt kind of embarrassed, being five seconds late on the blast. Drake was right on the button. Sharp character, old Drake. If all the brass were like him, a man wouldn't mind throwing a few salutes. Too bad the army hadn't been what he'd dreamed it would be: good men, trained fine, ready to face anything together, one for all and all for one, or whatever the old saying was. Corny, maybe, but it was still the best thing in the world, to be with the ones you knew you could count on. Funny, back home he'd believed all that crap he'd been brought up on, about how much better he was than the *goyim,* had thought a black man was one notch above a gorilla. That was one thing about the army; he'd found out that when the going got rough; it wasn't the religion or the hide that counted, it was the stuff inside. Like Drake. Drake was the best. And old Jess. They didn't make 'em any better. He'd go all the way to hell with those two—like now. He didn't like this job, not anything about it. Those civilians were no dumbbells, and they were scared all the way through. And Pyler, too. He was a bastard, but nobody had ever said he was yellow. But it was O.K. being here, knowing what to do, how to do it, knowing Jess was in it with him, that Drake was running the show. It was O.K. And it was time to get moving.

Weintraub flashed his needle-light around the big room, spotting the ladder against the wall behind the big sheet-metal duct, the trapdoor above it, right where they'd said. So far so good. All he had to do now was shin up there and get into the crawl-space, and head for the target.

But still he hesitated. It looked too easy. It was what the double-domes that worked in the place had figured out—but they hadn't done so hot when *they'd* been on the inside. Got their tails burned off. So maybe it might be a smart idea to take two looks at the layout before he jumped.

Weintraub worked the light over the walls, ceiling, and floor. He got to his feet, moved along the wall, not touching it. The back of the big air-handlers looked about the same as the front. There was a wooden ladder clamped against the rear wall, in a narrow space behind a big condenser. A square grille was set in the wall above it. There was nothing about it that looked any better than the other route, but Weintraub liked it better somehow. He lifted the ladder down, propped it against the wall, climbed it until he was facing the plastic grille. There were two plastic knobs holding it. He loosened them, swung the grille aside, and was looking into a dusty loft. Using his elbows, he pulled himself up and in. The light showed him a wide, low room, crammed full of ducting, conduits, cables, pipes. He didn't like the look of all that gear, but there wasn't much he could do about it. He knew which way to go. He started off, picking his way carefully over, under, and through the obstructions.

Ten minutes later, following his mental image of the diagrams he had studied for a full five minutes before starting out, he had reached the spot Drake had picked for him—he hoped. If he was on target, there would be a black pipe here as big as his leg. According to the civilians, it was some kind of lube conduit. When he blew it, it would shut down the high-pressure silicone supply to the generator bearings, and in about three minutes they'd overheat and kick in a set of automatic breakers. Anyway, that was the theory. It was plenty noisy here. That was a good sign. The manifold room was supposed to be right below him. And there was the pipe. He shone the light along the glazed black surface. The junction where it made a right-angle bend down looked like the spot to hit. Weintraub placed the light so as to shine on the angle and extracted the shaped charge from the pouch over his right hip. From another pocket he took the detonator, a tiny capsule half an inch long. He handled it with exaggerated care. The big charge would blow a hole through a concrete wall, but it stood a lot of handling. The cap, on the other hand, was as delicate as a cracked egg. One little slip, and *blam!*

He cut off that line of thought. Keep your mind on business, that was the secret. A guy who broke down and ran was just a guy who thought too much about the wrong things. He'd either finish the job and get out alive, or he wouldn't. If he didn't, he'd never know what hit him. So why worry? Smiling slightly, Ike Weintraub shifted position to get at the miniature tools clipped to his belt. His head struck a pipe passing low above him. It was not a hard blow, not really enough to daze him. But it was enough to jar the detonator cap from his fingers. It fell fourteen inches to the concrete floor and exploded with a force that shattered Weintraub's lower jaw and drove a sizable section of jagged bone into his jugular vein.

It was twenty-one seconds before his heart, having pumped the body's blood supply out through the immense wound, sucked convulsively on air, went into fibrillation, and stopped.

In the crawl-space above the switch room, big Jess Dooley heard the sharp report. He frowned, waiting for the howl of the screamer that would mean Drake or Ike had scored. But nothing came.

It figured. The bang hadn't been loud enough to be a working charge. Which left the question of what it *had* been. But that was a question that would have to wait. A category-one operation, Drake had said. That meant get the job done and ask questions later, at the corner table in the bar where the three of them did their serious drinking. Funny world. Couldn't get together in the NCO Club; Drake wasn't allowed. Same for the Officers' Club: no EM's wanted. Same for most of the joints off base: a black hide netted no smiles in the Main Street spots, and he'd have to whip half the draft-dodgers in darktown if he took a couple of Pinks down there. Yep, funny world. It was better here, with death crackling in the air all around him, doing the thing he knew how to do, with the men he knew he could count on to back his play, no matter what. Jess wiped sweat from his forehead with a thick finger, and using his pinpoint light, began studying the maze of conduits sprouting from the big panel on the wall, looking for the two that carried the wires to the thermostats that controlled the fuel supply to the nuclear generators buried a hundred feet below the station.

2

Falconer moved down from the boulder-strewn rim of the hollow, his eyes on the open, lighted doorway and on the slim shape soaring into darkness above.

"I searched for you, Xix," he said, in the old language that came haltingly to him. "I thought you'd lifted long ago, without me."

"I have never abandoned you, my commander," the voice called over the drum of rain. "So long as the Other knew my location, I would never be safe from him in my weakened condition. It was necessary that I conceal myself. But nine hours ago the natives erected a crude energy field on which I was able to draw for minimal functions. At once I sent out my call to you, my commander. We must act swiftly now."

Falconer laughed softly. "After all this time, Xix? What's your hurry?"

"Commander, the energy field is feeble, not matched to my receptors. I draw but a trickle of power from it, insufficient to charge my static-energy coil. If I am to lift from this planet, I require more power—much more."

"How long will it take to draw enough from the broadcast field?"

"Over a century. We cannot wait. We must charge the coil directly from the source, unattenuated by distance."

"How?"

"With your assistance, my commander. You must remove the lift coil, take it to the transmitting station, and tap the beam directly."

"It occurs to me that we're very close to the transmitter. That must have been the installation I saw on the way here. Rather a coincidence, eh, Xix?"

"Indeed, Commander. But the coil must be charged, and time is short. Already I have been forced to . . . But no matter. You must remove the coil and descend at once to the transmitter."

"I heard firing down there. What's going on, Xix?"

"An effort was made to shut down the transmission. Of course I cannot permit that."

"How can you stop it?"

"My commander, we must not delay now for discussion of peripheral matters. I sense that I am threatened; the hour for action has come."

Falconer crossed the rock-strewn ground, aware of the thunder and roll of the storm beyond the protected area sealed off by the ship's defensive field. He stepped up through the entry port, went along the dustless passage walled with smooth synthetic, ornamented with fittings of imperishable metal. In the control compartment, soft lights glowed across the banked dials and levers, so once-familiar, so long-forgotten.

"Xix—what about Gralgrathor? If he's still alive—"

"The traitor is dead."

"So many years," he said. "I don't feel any hate any longer." He laughed, not a jolly laugh. "I don't feel much of anything."

"Soon you will, my commander. The long twilight ends. Ysar waits for us."

"Yes," Falconer said. "Now I'd better get busy. It's been a long time since I put a tool to a machine of Ysar."

3

John Zabisky, wounded in the lower right side by a steel-jacketed thirty-caliber slug which had broken a rib, punctured a lung, traversed his liver, and lodged in the inner curve of the ilium, lay on his face under a dense-needled dwarf pine. Immediately after he had been shot, he had covered fifty feet of rough going in his initial plunge away from danger before the shock had overtaken him and dropped him on his face. For a while then—he had no idea how long—he had lain, dazed, feeling the hot, spreading ache in his side grow into a throbbing agony that swelled inside him like a ravenous animal feeding on his guts. Then the semieuphoric state had given way to full consciousness. Zabisky explored with his fingers, found the entry wound. It was bleeding, but not excessively. The pain seemed to be somewhere else, deep inside. He was gut-shot, bleeding internally. He knew what that meant. He had an hour, maybe two. A lousy way to go out. He lay with his cheek against the mud and thought about it.

Why the hell had he followed the guy, Falconer, after he'd kissed him off? He had his money, two cees. Curiosity? Not exactly that; it was more than just sticking his nose in. It was like the guy needed him—like he was mixed up in something too tough for him, trying to do it alone, tackling too much for one man. And you wanted to help the guy, stick by him. It was like there was something at stake, something you couldn't put in words; but if you finked out, let it slide, washed your hands of it, you'd never be able to see yourself again as the man you thought you were. It was like in the old days, kind of, when the first John Sobieski had climbed on his horse and led his men into battle. It was a thing you had to do, or admit you were nothing.

Yeah. And then the light had hit him in the face, and some guy yells, and then the ballbat hit him in the side, and he heard the gun firing after him, and then he was here, and what good were the two cees now?

And where the hell was here? Halfway up some lousy hill, in the woods, in the middle of the night, in a storm like you didn't see twice in one lifetime.

Especially not his lifetime. Maybe another hour. Maybe not that much.

Falconer would help him, if he knew.

Falconer was up ahead, someplace.

Got to get moving.

Painfully, grunting, fighting back the nausea and the weakness, Zabisky pulled himself forward another foot. He had covered perhaps a hundred yards when he saw the glow above. That would be Falconer up there. Probably had a cabin up there, a warm room, a fire, a bed. Better to die in a bed than here. Better to die just trying for it than to stop here and let the pain wash up and up until it covered you and you sank down in it and were like all the other extinct animals you saw in books. Not much you could do then, about anything. But it hadn't come to that yet. Not quite. He still had a few yards left in him. Take 'em one at a time, that was the trick. One at a time ... as long as time held out.

He had covered another half-dozen yards when he heard the sound above: a faint clatter of a dislodged pebble.

"Falconer," he called, peering upward. There was a movement there, among the shadows. A long, high-shouldered, narrow shape flowed into view, stood looking down with yellow eyes that seemed to blaze like tiny fires against the blackness.

4

Two hundred yards to the east and a hundred feet below, Grayle worked his way along the face of a weathered fissure in the rock. Three times he had attempted to gain the ledge above; three times he had fallen back. The distance was too great, the scant handholds too slippery, the broken ribs still too crippling. Now he descended to the talus below, angling to the south, skirting the barrier. The grade was less precipitate here; stunted trees had found footholds; brush and exposed roots offered grips for his hands. He made more rapid progress, moving laterally into bigger timber. Striking a faint path, he turned right along it, resumed his ascent. He had covered only a few yards when he saw the body lying at the base of the pine.

For long seconds he stood staring down at the ripped throat of the dead man. Then he made an animal noise deep in his throat, shook himself like a man waking from a nightmare, and started upward.

He had covered a hundred yards when he heard sounds ahead: the grate of feet on stone, the puffing of labored breath. More than one man, making clumsy progress upward.

He left the path and hurried to overtake them.

5

Lying flat on his back in utter darkness, Sergeant Jess Dooley felt the miniature power hacksaw cut through the second of the two conduits. It had been a delicate operation, cutting all the way around each of the half-inch stainless-steel tubes without touching the wires inside, but the engineers had made it pretty plain what would happen if a man shorted them accidentally.

Now the trick was to short them on purpose and get away in one piece. Dooley wiped sweat on his forearm and thought about the layout he had studied on paper. Memory was important to a man in his line of work. You had to have a natural mnemonic aptitude, and then survive some tough training to qualify as a member of a Special Team. After all the trouble of getting to where the job was, there were plenty of times when completing it depended on perfect recall of a complicated diagram.

Like now. It wouldn't do to just cut a wire; there were six back-up systems that would take over in that case— even if he wasn't fried in the process. He had to tinker the thing to give a false reading—and not too false at that. Just enough to show a no-demand condition, and make the automatic cutouts lock in. These automated layouts were pretty smart; they could deal with just about any situation that came up. But you could fool 'em. They didn't expect to get a phony signal from their own guts.

And if he could attach the little gadget the technical boys had handed him at just the right spot, in just the right way—between sensors, and if possible at the same instant as a legitimate impulse from the thermostats . . .

Well, then, he might get away with it.

He extracted the device—the size of a worm pill for a medium-sized dog—removed the protective tubing from the contacts. He shifted position, settling himself so he could make one smooth, coordinated motion. The protective devices wouldn't like it if he fumbled the hook-on, making and breaking contact half a dozen times in half a second before he got the ringer in position.

He was ready. Sweat was running down into his eyes. He wiped at it ineffectively with his shoulder. Hot in here, no air. A man could suffocate before he got the job done. So what was he waiting for? Nothing. He was ready. The next time the relay clicked—it cycled about once every five minutes—he'd make his move.

6

Captain Zwicky, a few feet in advance of Sergeant Pitcher and Lieutenant Harmon, pulled himself up over an outcropping of granite and started to rise to his feet.

"That's far enough, Captain," a deep voice said from above. "This is no place for you tonight. Go back."

Zwicky remained frozen, both hands and one knee on the ground, an expression of total astonishment on his upturned face. Behind him, Pitcher, hearing the sudden voice, halted, then eased forward. Over the captain's shoulder he could see dark underbrush, dripping foliage— and the legs and torso of a man. A big man, in dark clothes.

In a single motion, he raised the carbine, sighted, and fired. At the explosion beside his right ear, Zwicky plunged forward and sideways. Pitcher, his path cleared, scrambled up, saw the tall, dark-shadowed figure still standing in the same position; hastily, he brought the carbine up—and felt a ringing shock against his hands as the gun flew from his grip. He made a lunge in the direction the weapon had skidded, felt hard hands catch him, lift him, turn him. Zwicky was on his feet, raising his carbine; but he was having trouble finding a clear shot. Pitcher felt himself swung forward, released. He crashed downward through twenty feet of brush before he came up hard against a tree. As he struggled up, Lieutenant Harmon grabbed his arm, dragged him to his feet.

"What happened up there? That shot—"

"Leggo," Pitcher blurted. He chopped at Harmon's hand, grabbed for the other's pistol. "Gimme that—"

"You nuts—"

The arrival of Captain Zwicky, sliding and tumbling down the trail, cut off his protest. Pitcher stepped back, holding the pistol, as Zwicky came to rest on his back between the two men.

"Stand fast, Sergeant!" he blurted as Pitcher started past him.

"I'm getting the bastard that killed Obers," Pitcher snarled.

"That's an order!" Pitcher halted as Zwicky crawled to his feet. His nose was bleeding, and he had lost his cap. He wiped at his face with the back of his hand, smearing blood which ran down, mingling with rainwater.

"Losing more men won't help anything," he said. "I

don't know what we're up against, but it's more than it looks like. Before we try it again, we have to—"

At that moment, a sound cut through the crash of the storm: a strident, wailing scream that ran down the scale and died in a groan of horror.

Without a word, Harmon whirled and plunged down the path. Pitcher backed two steps, was jabbed between the shoulderblades by the stub of a dead branch. He dropped his carbine, dived down the slope head-first. Zwicky hesitated for a moment, started to shout a command, then turned and went down the path, not running, but wasting no time.

7

"What in the Nine Hells was that?" Falconer rose from the open panel behind which the compact bulk of the drained energy coil was mounted.

"Don't be alarmed," the cool voice of the ship said. "It is merely a warning device. I arranged to keep the native life in all its forms at a distance."

"It sounded like a hunting *krill*. By the king of all devils, I'd forgotten that sound."

"It serves its purpose most effectively—"

"What set it off just now?"

"A native was prowling nearby."

"A strange time and place to be prowling."

"Have no fear; now that my Y-field is restored, I am safe from their petty mischief."

"I may have led them here," Falconer said. "It's too bad. There's likely to be trouble when I start back down."

"There are weapons in my armory, commander—"

"I have no desire to murder anyone, Xix," Falconer said. "These are people too; this is their world."

"Commander, you are as far above these natives as—

but I distract you from your task. Their presence nearby indicates the need for haste."

In silence, Falconer resumed the disassembly of the lift unit.

8

For a moment after the cry of the hunting *krill* sounded, Grayle stood staring upward into the darkness of the rim beyond which faint light gleamed on the slanting curtain of rain. There was no further sound. He resumed his climb, crossed a slope of naked rock, made his way up over a jumble of granite, and was looking across a pebble-strewn ledge at the soft glowing U1-metal hull of a fleet boat of the Ysarian navy upreared among the rock slabs.

9

Jess Dooley heard the soft click of the relay as it opened. He had precisely 0.4 second to move. In a smooth motion, he touched the two wires of the false-signal device to the exposed conductors. A spark jumped to the exposed end of the cut-through conduit, from which a volatile antistatic and coolant fluid was draining. The flash of fire seared the hair from the left side of Dooley's scalp, charred the edge of his ear, scorched deep into the exposed skin of his neck. In instant reflex, the man snatched a tiny high-pressure can from his belt, directed a billow of smothering foam at himself, at the pool of fluid over which pale blue flames leaped like burning brandy on a fruitcake, over the conduits and cables around him. He moved backward, awkward under the low ceiling, holding his breath to exclude the mixture of flame, foam, and noxious gases.

The flames winked and dimmed. Then the pain hit.

Dooley dropped the can, groped for another, gave himself a liberal dose of nerve paralyzant. The burned side of his face went wooden. Too late, he turned his head. A drop of condensed painkiller trickled down into the corner of his right eye. There was a momentary stinging; then numbness, darkness.

Swearing to himself, Dooley found his needle-light, switched it on. Nothing. The light was hot against his hand. It was working, all right. But he couldn't see it. With nerve-deadener in both eyes, he was blind as a bat.

Nice work, Dooley. Nice spot. Is the fire out? Hope so. Is the little magic combination can-opener and disaster-averter in place and functioning? Hope that too. Meanwhile, how does a man go about getting the hell out of here?

Alone, in darkness, Dooley began inching his way back along the route he had come.

In the glow of the campfire, the faces of the men are ruddy, belying the privations of the long campaign. They sit in silence, listening to the shrill of cicadas, the soft sounds of the river, looking across at the scattered lights of Vicksburg.

An orderly approaches, a boy scarcely out of his teens, thin and awkward in his dusty blue uniform. He halts before a broad-shouldered officer with shoulder-length hair, once red, now shot with gray.

"General Logan, Major Tate's compliments, sir, and they took a rebel colonel half an hour ago scouting this side of the river, and would the general like to talk to him."

The big man rises. "All right, lad." He follows the boy along the crooked path among the pitched tents where men in rumpled blue sit restlessly, oppressed by the humid heat and the swarming insects. At a rough compound built of boards wrenched from the walls of a nearby barn, a slouching sentry straightens as they approach, presents arms. A captain emerges from a tent, salutes, speaks to an armed sergeant. A detail of four men falls in beside them. The gate is opened.

"A five-man escort?" General Logan says mildly as they enter the compound. "He must be a redoubtable warrior indeed."

The captain has a round red face, a long, straggly moustache. He wipes sweat from his face, nods.

"A hard case. Powell swears he broke a half-inch rope they had on him. I guess if he hadn't been out cold when they found him, they wouldn't have got the rope on him in the first place. I'm taking no chances with him."

They halt before a blacksmith's forge, where a bare-headed man stands, trussed with new hemp rope. He is big, broad, with a square, scarred face and black-red hair. There are iron manacles on his wrists; an iron cannonball lies by, in position to be attached to his left ankle. There is blood on his face and on his gray tunic.

General Logan stares at the man. "You," he says in a tone of profound astonishment. The prisoner blinks through the dried blood which has run down into his eyes. Abruptly, he makes a shrugging motion, and the men holding him are thrown back. He tenses, and with a sharp popping sound, the hemp strands break. He reaches, seizes the blacksmith's hammer in his manacled hands, leaps forward, and brings the heavy sledge down with smashing force on the skull of the Union general.

Chapter Thirteen

1

Carrying the heavy coil, Falconer stood for a moment in the entry, looking out across the circle of dry dust and loose stone soft-lit by the ship's port lights, ending in abrupt transition to the rim of broken, rain-swept rock, and beyond, the tops of black trees rising from below.

"Good luck, Commander," Xix said as he stepped down. Burdened by the heavy load, he picked his way across toward the point below which the path led downward. He had descended less than a hundred feet when he saw the man lying face-down in the path, bulky in a bright-colored mackinaw. Falconer dropped the coil, knelt by the man's side. There was blood on the side of the heavy coat. He turned the man over, saw the gaping wounds across the side of the thick, muscular neck, the shredded front of the sodden jacket.

"John Zabisky," he muttered. "Why did you follow me?"

Zabisky's eyelids stirred, lifted; his small, opal-black eyes looked into Falconer's. His lips moved.

"I . . . tried," he said distinctly; then all the light went out of his eyes, left them as dull as stones.

Falconer rose, stood looking down at the rain falling on the face of the dead man. He glanced up at a faint sound, and a hard white light struck him in the eyes.

"I should have known you wouldn't die," a deep, harsh voice said out of the darkness.

2

"So you're alive, Gralgrathor," Falconer said.

Grayle came forward, looked at the body on the ground at Falconer's feet. "I see you've had a busy night, Lokrien."

"And more business yet to come. I don't have time to waste, Thor. Go your way and I'll go mine—or are you still intent on braining me?"

"I didn't come here to kill you, Lokrien. My business is with *that*." He tilted his head toward the faint glow from above.

"You expect Xix to take you off this world?"

"On the contrary: Xix isn't going anywhere."

"I think he is. Stand aside, Thor."

"I didn't come to kill you, Loki," Grayle said. "But I will if you try to interfere." He pointed down the path. "You'll be safe down there—"

"We'll go down together."

"You're going down. I'm going up," Grayle said.

Falconer shook his head. "No," he said.

Grayle looked across at him, his square face obscure in the darkness. "When the Y-field went on and I felt the homing pulse, I knew you'd come, if you lived. I hoped to get here ahead of you. It's strange, but over the years the thought had grown in my mind that somehow, in some way, there'd been some fantastic mistake. Then I saw the dead man down below. I knew then I'd find you here."

"I find that remark obscure, Thor."

"Have you forgotten I've seen wounds like those before?"

"Indeed? Where, might I ask?

"You dare to ask me that—"

Soft footfalls sounded, coming closer. From the shadows beside the path, a sinuous shape emerged, pacing on padded feet. It resembled, more than any other terrestrial creature, a giant black panther: as big as a Bengal tiger, but longer-legged, slimmer, deeper-chested, with a round skull and bright, alert yellow eyes. It advanced on Grayle, raised a claw-studded paw as big as a dinner plate. . . .

"Stop!" Falconer shouted, and leaped between the man and the beast. The *krill* halted, lashed its tail, seated itself on its haunches.

"Do not be alarmed, Lokrien," it said in the smooth, carefully modulated voice of Xix. "I am here to help you."

3

"What are you?" Falconer said. "Where do you come from?"

"My appearance must surprise you, Commander," the cat-thing said. "But I am a construct, nothing more."

"An Ysarian construct. How?"

"Xix created me. I am his eyes and ears at a distance. You may address him through me." The *krill* rose, paced a step toward Grayle.

"Leave him alone," Falconer said.

The *krill* stared at Falconer. "My commander, the traitor must die."

"I need his help to force an entry into the plant."

"Nonsense—"

"That's an order, Xix!" Falconer faced Grayle. "Drop the grenade belt. Pick up the coil." He indicated the latter lying where he had left it.

"This thing belongs to you, eh, Loki?" Grayle eyed the *krill*. "I wondered why you chose the particular method you did—but now that I've seen your weapon, I under-stand."

"Commander—let me kill the traitor!" the *krill* hissed.

Falconer looked into the yellow eyes.

"Are you the only construct Xix made?"

"There were others, Commander."

"Not in the shape of animals . . ."

"True."

"A man named Pinquelle . . . and Riuies . . . and a soldier called Sleet . . ."

"I have had many names, Commander."

"Why? Why didn't you announce yourself?"

"It seemed wiser to be discrete. As for my purpose—why, it was to assist you in the nurture of the technology we needed to do that which we must do."

"The placement of the power plant is no coincidence, then."

"I was instrumental in selecting the site, yes."

"You're full of surprises, aren't you . . . Xix? I wonder what you'll come up with next."

"I am true to my purpose, Commander, nothing more."

Falconer turned abruptly to Grayle.

"We're going down the mountain, Thor. We're going to recharge the power coil and return here. Then Xix is going to lift for Ysar. Help me, and I'll take you with me; refuse, and Xix will deal with you."

Grayle growled and took a step toward him. The *krill* tensed its long legs, its head up, eyes bright on Grayle's throat. Falconer stared into Grayle's face.

"Why, Thor?" he said softly. "Why are you intent on destroying us all?"

"I swore to kill you, Loki. I intend to fulfill that promise."

The *krill* yowled and yearned toward Grayle; Falconer restrained it with a word. "You can commit suicide," he said. "Whereas if you stay alive and cooperate, a better opportunity may present itself."

For a moment Grayle hesitated. Then he stepped back,

picked up the coil, slung it by its straps over his shoulder.

"Yes," he said. "Perhaps it will."

4

Colonel Ajax Pyler stood beside his staff car, looking toward the point from which the firing had come.

"Well, Cal? What the devil is going on over there!"

The aide was speaking urgently into a field phone: "Bring him up to the road. I'll talk to him myself." He switched off. "A B Company man, Colonel; something spooked him. He swears he saw two men cross the plant grounds and enter the building. He opened up on them. . . ."

"And?"

"It's a wild tale . . . here they come now."

A jeep was approaching from the direction of the perimeter fence. It pulled in beside the staff car; a sergeant and a private jumped down, stood at attention. The sergeant saluted.

"Sir, this is the private—"

"I can see that. Get on with it. Just what did you see, soldier?"

"Colonel, I seen these here two fellers, they come out o' the woods up above where I was at; first thing I knew he had my gun out of my hands—"

"Were you asleep?"

"Not me, Colonel, too damn cold, these fellers come up quiet, and with the wind and all, and I was watching toward the plant, never figured nobody—"

"So they jumped you and took your gun. Then what?"

"Well—I guess I yelled, and one of 'em told me to be quiet. Real nice-spoken, he was. Big feller. Both of 'em. And—"

"What happened, man? Which way did they go?"

"Why, like I told sergeant here, they up and went right down through the wire—"

"What did they cut it with?"

"Hell, Colonel, they didn't cut nothing. Tore that wire up with their bare hands. One of 'em did. Other feller was loaded down—"

"Sergeant, why didn't the alarms go off? I ordered triple circuitry all the way around the perimeter!"

"Colonel, I don't know—"

"How could anyone get inside unobserved? The entrance is floodlit—"

"That's just it, Colonel! They never used the front door—nor the holes them Special Forces boys blew. Just walked right through the wall! And after come this critter. Big, black as a caved-in coal mine, and eyes like fire. It come right up to me and looked at me like hell's door left open, and went on down and through the wire—that was when I let fly, Colonel. I—"

"That's enough!" Pyler jerked his head at the sergeant. "Take this man back to the dispensary. I don't know what he's been drinking, or where he got it, but he's raving like a lunatic."

He turned to his aide. "Cal, get a squad of master marksmen together, post them covering the exit. If there's anyone in there, we'll be ready when he comes out!"

5

Lieutenant Harmon pushed through the clump of men examining the tangled barbed wire through which a swath had been untidily cut.

". . . look at these ends," a man was saying. "That wasn't sheared, it failed in tension. Look at the deformation. It's been stretched."

"Hey—here's why the screamers didn't go off." Another man showed a strand of insulated wire. "They jumped it."

"Who saw what happened?" Harmon barked the question. Faces turned his way. He got a brief second- and third-hand account of the progress of the two intruders through the wire, across the grounds, and into the rear of the building.

"They didn't mess with the doors," a bulky corporal grunted. "They made their own hole."

"What's that supposed to mean?"

"Put the light on it, Sherm," the corporal said. A dazzling searchlight sprang to brilliance, thrust a smoky finger across the hundred yards of rain-soaked turf to glare on the buff-colored masonry wall marred by a ragged black aperture at ground level.

"I didn't hear any explosion," Harmon said.

"Wasn't none." The corporal spat. "They busted that hole bare-handed."

"Don't kid me," Harmon snarled.

"Hey, ain't you that out-of-state cop?" A freckle-faced soldier with a pale, pinched face spoke up. "I heard the man you were after tore the door off a car, something like that. Maybe it's the same guy."

Harmon glowered at the laughter. "Where'd they take this kid that saw all this?"

"Field dispensary. Down the road."

Harmon walked back to the jeep Zwicky had lent him, turned it, drove back up past the parked vehicles of the convoy. It took him fifteen minutes to find the white mobile hospital, parked in a field under trees. Inside, he asked for and was led to Tatum's bedside.

"Hell, I ain't sick," the private said indignantly.

"Take it easy, fellow," Harmon said. "Now tell me what this man you saw looked like. . . ."

6

Lying in darkness with his face against the cool floor, Jess Dooley drew deep, regular breaths, forcing himself back to calm. Panic wasn't going to help. Panic kills, that was what the posters on the cool, green walls back at headquarters said. He wasn't really trapped in a maze with no way out, trapped in the dark, buried alive—

Nothing like that. He was lost, sure. A man could get lost easy enough in a mess of crawlways, even if he *had* studied the plans for a whole five minutes. But what was lost could be found. All he had to do was keep his head, feel his way, and after a while he'd hear them coming to look for him. He'd been scraping his chin and bumping his head and eating dust and taking the long tour of the crawlway system for half an hour now. Been doing all right, too, up until the panic hit him. Claustrophobia, that's what they called it. Never bothered him before. But thirty minutes of being blind was enough for the first time out. Now he wanted air, wanted light, wanted to raise his head, stand up, instead of being crushed in here in this space just high enough to push through, with all those tons of rock above—

Take it easy, Dooley. No panic, remember? Maybe one of the other guys had gotten in first and forgotten to fire his screamer, and maybe it was all just spinned wheels.

And maybe he'd better stop laying here and get moving. Jess snorted dust from his nose and moved forward. His outstretched hand touched a rounded plastic-walled duct. He remembered the duct system: it would lead a man out of this maze. And there were access panels spotted along it. . . .

Three minutes later, Dooley was inside the big duct, headed in a direction he hoped was upstream. He covered fifty feet, rounded a turn—and heard faint sounds from up ahead—or was it off to the side? Voices. Good old Drake, knew he'd come, him and Ike. Close now. Yell, and let them know? Hell with it. Came this far, play it cool. Could see a faint light up ahead, through a grille. Dope was wearing off. Just make it up there, and flap a hanky, and in another minute or two they'd be outside, having a good laugh together, breathing that cold, fresh air. . . . Smiling, Jess Dooley moved forward along the duct above the Energy Staging Room.

The exhaust grille was a louvered panel two feet by three, designed to be serviced from the inside. Jess found the release clips, lifted the grid aside. The voices were clearer now, not more than twenty, thirty feet away. . . .

Jess frowned, listening. That wasn't Drake's voice, or Ike's. They weren't even speaking English. Frowning, Jess lay in the darkness and listened.

7

"Put it down here," Falconer ordered. Grayle lowered the drained power coil to the floor, while the *krill* watched closely.

Falconer knelt beside the pack, unstrapped it, exposing the compact device within.

"Get the cover off the service hatch," he ordered.

Followed by the cat-thing, Grayle crossed to the hatch, forced a finger under the edge of the steel plate, ripped it away as if it were wet cardboard.

"Stand aside," Falconer lifted the discharged coil. Grayle hadn't moved.

"Don't try it yet," Falconer said. "The odds are still too great."

"Loki, don't charge that coil," Grayle said. "Defy your master; without your help, it's powerless."

"My master . . . ?"

The *krill* moved swiftly forward, raised a hook-studded forearm.

"Stand fast, Xix," Falconer snapped. The creature paused, turned its great eyes on him. "He threatens our existence, Commander."

"I'll decide that."

"But will you?" Grayle said. "Don't you really know yet, Loki?"

The *krill* yowled and struck at Grayle, ripping the leather arm of his jacket as he jumped back. It followed, ignoring Falconer's shout.

"See how your faithful slave comes to heel, Loki!" Grayle called.

Falconer took two swift steps to the open hatch, poised the coil on the rim, caught up the two heavy jack-tipped cables.

"Stop, Xix—or I'll cross-connect the coil and melt it down to slag!"

The *krill* whirled on Falconer, jaws gaping, the serrated bony ridges that served as teeth bared in a snarl.

"Would you aid the treacher in his crimes?"

"I'll listen to what he has to say," Falconer said.

"Commander—remember: only I can take you back to Ysar!"

"Talk, Thor," Falconer said. "What are you hinting at?"

8

Twelve feet to the right and eight feet above the spot where Grayle stood with his back to the wall, Jess Dooley lay, his blind eyes staring into inky blackness, his ears straining to make sense of the jabber of alien voices rising through the open ventilation grille beside him.

There were three of them: one deep, rough-edged, one a resonant baritone, one an emotionless tenor. He didn't like that last one: it sounded the way a corpse would sound if it could sit up and talk. And the other two sounded mad clear through. Jess couldn't understand the words, but he knew the tone. Somebody was fixing to kill somebody down there. There wasn't any way he could stop it, even if the victim didn't have it coming. Because this was them, sure enough: the ones who'd messed things up here, sabotaged the place, killed all those people. Russians, probably. Too bad he didn't know Russian. Probably be getting an earful now.

He was lucky he'd heard them when he did. Another second, and he'd have dropped right down amongst 'em. And from what he'd heard about Commie spies, that would be the end of the Dooley biography.

No, there was nothing to do. Just lie quiet and wait for what came next—and be ready to move fast, if it worked out that way.

9

Lying on the hard cot in the tiny-walled room, Anne Rogers wondered where she was. She remembered wind, rain, bright lights shining across wet tarmac—

They had taken a helicopter. She and . . . and a man. . . .

It was gone again. A crazy dream. About running, and police cars, shots, breaking glass—

The copter, hurtling low above whipping treetops, the sudden jarring impact, and—

She had been hurt. Maybe the copter ride was a dream, but she had been hurt. She was sure of that. Her hands went to her face, explored her skull, checked her arms, ribs; she sat up and was surprised at the dizziness that swept over her. Her legs seemed to be intact; there were no heavy bandages swathing her anywhere. Her head ached, and there were lesser aches here and there; but nothing serious. Her eyes went once again around the small room. A hospital, of course. Some sort of temporary one, like the kind the police took to the scene of an accident—

The police. She remembered all about the police now. He—the man—strange, she couldn't remember his face clearly, or his name—had attacked a policeman—or two of them. And now where was he? Anne felt a sudden pang of fear. Was he dead? For some reason, the idea filled her with panic. She swung her legs over the side of the bed. She was still fully dressed, even to the muddy trenchcoat. Whoever had brought her here hadn't taken much trouble with her. But why should they? As far as they were concerned, she was just a gun moll—an accomplice of an escaped convict.

Rain drummed and beat on the roof, only inches above her head. She rose, went, a little unsteadily, across to the narrow door. A passage less than three feet wide led past identical doors to a square of dim light at the end. She went to it, looked through a window into a room where a man stood talking into a canvas-cased telephone.

" . . . he's inside the power plant, Captain, but I can't get any cooperation out of the army. I've been ordered to stay the hell and gone back from the fence, not go near the place. But this boy is my meat, Brasher, all six-three of him! I've got bones to pick with this con, and it'll be *his* bones!" There was a pause while he listened, his face set in a scowl.

"Don't worry, I know how to handle it. . . . Sure, I'll stay back. I've got the spot all picked. I can cover the front and the hole he blasted in the side, both. Whichever way he comes, I'll be there—just for insurance. I'll be watching him through the sights. One wrong move, and— Sure, I'll watch it. Don't sweat me, Captain—just so I've got your backing. Right." He hung up, stood smiling a crooked smile at the wall.

"But I've got a funny feeling," he said softly, aloud, "that any move that son of a bitch makes will be the wrong one—for him!"

Anne moved quickly away from the door, hurried to the opposite end of the passage, stepped out into driving wind and slashing rain. It was dark here, but a hundred feet away were the lights of the vehicles on the road, and beyond was the looming pile of the power plant, bleak as a mortuary in the glare of the floodlights.

Grayle was in there. And when he came out, they'd be waiting for him. She had to warn him. There had to be a way. . . .

Ten minutes later, having crossed the road below the convoy and approached the power plant beyond the glare of the field lights, Anne studied the front of the building from the shelter of a clump of alders. The doors had been blown away, the entry was wide open. There was nobody near it. If she ran, without stopping to think, quickly, now—

She had covered half of the hundred yards of open lawn before a shout sounded.

"It's a woman!" another voice yelled.

"Shoot, damn you!" a third voice commanded.

There was the flat, echoing *carrong!* of a heavy rifle, and mud leaped in a gout beside her. She ran on, heard the second shot, felt the sting of mud that spattered her legs. Then she was among the rubble, leaping an overturned chair, scrambling between broken door frames as a third bullet chipped stone above her head and screamed away into darkness.

"Grayle," Anne whispered, looking along the dark corridor. "Where are you?"

Five minutes later she came on wet, muddy footprints in the passage. She followed them, moving quickly along the silent passage, to a stairwell leading down.

10

"Do you know what my mission here on Earth was, Loki?" Grayle asked.

"To conduct a routine reconnaissance—"

"One of Xix's lies. My orders were to establish a Class O beacon."

"Class O—that refers to a major navigational aid with a power output in the lower stellar range."

"Commonly known as a Hellcore."

"A Hellcore device—on an inhabited world?" Falconer shook his head. "You must be mistaken. Battle Command has no authority to order such a measure."

"The order didn't come from Battle Command. It came from Praze—my ship."

"Go on."

"I refused to comply, ordered the mission aborted. Praze refused, overrode my commands."

"I wondered about the crash. An Ysarian ship doesn't malfunction. You scuttled her, didn't you?"

"Ship-killer!" the *krill* hissed.

"I scuttled her—but not before she got the Hellcore away. It impacted in the sea, off the coast of the continent now known as North America."

"Why didn't you refer the order to Battle Command for confirmation?"

"Battle Command is a machine. It would have confirmed it."

"You're raving, Thor. Battle Command is made up of veteran combat officers: High General Wotan, Admiral Tyrr—"

"No, Loki—not for a long time now. You might ask Xix how long."

"Commander—we will listen no longer to this treacher! Charge the coil! Our time runs out!"

"Ask him what his hurry is, Loki. Ask him what it is he's so eager to accomplish."

"To leave this world, what else?" the *krill* said.

"Ask him about the beacon."

"What does the beacon have to do with it?"

"He raves, my commander," the *krill* whined.

"Ask him about the storm," Grayle said. "Ask him what he had to do with that!"

Falconer looked across at the great black entity. "Answer," he said.

"Very well—but we waste precious seconds. My instruments told me that the beacon device had been placed on the surface, but only the basic protective field was energized, due to the sabotage of the traitor. My first act when I began to draw energy from the primitive broadcast field was to transmit the 'proceed' signal on the Y-band for crust penetration, using a matter-annihilation beam. Naturally, a side effect of weather disturbance was created. The device is now well within the planetary interior. Once we are clear of the planet, it will require only the final triggering pulse to the reactor to ignite the beacon. But we must act swiftly! If the triggering signal is not received within a period of hours, the device self-destructs!"

"Cancel that," Falconer said. "We're not going to activate the beacon. It won't be needed now—not after all these years."

"Not perform our clear duty?"

"It's not our duty—not anymore."

"I fail to understand what circumstances you conceive could relieve us of responsibility for completion of a Fleet mission."

"Time—a great deal of time has passed. If the beacon had been needed, another ship would have been sent out."

"How does the passage of a few days influence the Ysarian Grand Strategy?"

"Over twelve hundred local years is more than a few days."

"What is this talk of centuries? Is it perhaps intended as a jest?"

"Don't you know how long we've been here?"

"Since our arrival at this world, less than ten thousand hours have elapsed; a little over a year."

"Something's interfered with your chronometry, Xix. You're wrong by a factor of a thousand."

"I am incapable of error within my design parameters. The need for the beacon is as great as ever. Accordingly, I will trigger it as planned. I can agree with no other course."

"*You* can agree? You're a machine. You follow my orders."

"My ultimate responsibility is to Battle Command. Its directives override your authority, Commander. The beacon will be activated as planned. Let us hope that the White Fleet has not suffered reverses in battle for lack of it."

"I think I understand," Falconer said. "Xix, you've been on Q status for most of the past twelve centuries. Your chronometric sensors only registered the periods of awareness."

"It is correct that I have from time to time reverted to J status as a power-conservation measure. But I fail to grasp your implication that this status has dimensional characteristics."

"It means," Grayle said, "that as far as it's concerned, when it's switched off, nothing is happening."

"The phenomenal world exists only during active status," Xix said calmly. "This is confirmed not only by basic rationality, but by the absence of sensory input during such periods."

"I see: you don't shut yourself off—you turn off the world."

"These are mere semantic niceties, my commander—".

"How do you account for the fact that when you reactivate, you find that changes have taken place around you?"

"I have observed that it is a characteristic of the universe to reform in somewhat altered state after a discontinuity."

"What about the power broadcast you're drawing on? You think the savages I found here a millennium ago could have built that transmitter in six weeks?"

"A manifestation of the discontinuity effect previously noted. I had intended to discuss these phenomena with you at leisure, possibly during the voyage home."

"Do you realize," Falconer said, "that when you transmit that signal you'll turn the planet into a minor sun?"

"That is correct," the *krill* said.

"For the love of Ysar, Xix—listen to me—"

"For the love of Ysar, my commander, I cannot. Now, let me proceed with that which must be done."

"Tell it to go to the Ninth Hell," Grayle said thickly.

"Come, my commander—you know that without the coil I—and you—can never leave this world—and time grows short."

"Don't do it, Loki," Grayle said. "Let the ship rot where it is."

The *krill* seemed to smile at Falconer, baring a serrated ridge of ivory white. "Without power, I cannot lift, true. But I will not come to an end by slow decay—nor by the chemical bombs of the primitives. Reflect: the Y-field is still at operational level, is it not? I can trigger the beacon at any moment—from here."

"And incinerate yourself along with the rest of the planet."

"I have no alternative but to perform my duty. Your

betrayal will change nothing—except that you will not live to see Ysar. I will regret your death. A useless death, Lokrien."

"If I agree," Falconer said, "will you contact a Fleet outpost for confirmation before you trigger the Hell-core?"

"It will mean a dangerous delay—but—yes, as you wish. I agree."

"It's lying," Grayle said. "As it's lied all along."

"Enough!" the *krill* said, rising to all fours. "Proceed, now, my commander! I can wait no longer!"

As Falconer hesitated, there was a sudden sharp sound from the door twenty feet distant in the end wall. It swung open, and a slim figure in a trench coat stepped through, hesitated. Her eyes found Grayle. In that instant, the *krill* crouched, leaped. Even more swiftly, Grayle moved, sprang between the beast and the girl. The *krill* struck him full on, knocked him back against the girl. She fell under their feet as Grayle rose, his hands locked on the beast's throat, while its talons raked him.

"Xix!" Falconer roared, and the cat-thing crouched away, while Grayle staggered, blood flooding down across his shredded jacket.

"You asked me once . . . where I'd seen wounds like those before," he said between his clenched teeth. "I thought then you mocked me."

"I saw John Zabisky," Falconer said. "And the dead soldier on the trail."

"There was another time . . . long ago, Loki. In a house built of timbers on a rocky hill among the snows. A woman and a child. Gudred, my wife, and Loki, my son." He looked across at Falconer. "May the Nine Gods forgive me, I thought you'd made them."

Falconer's face turned to a rigid mask. His eyes locked with those of the *krill*.

"*You* killed them," he said. "And let Thor believe I did it."

"It was necessary," the *krill* hissed. "He would have subverted you from your duty!"

"In the name of Ysar, you've betrayed everything that Ysar ever meant!"

"Ysar!" the *krill* yowled. "I weary of the name of Ysar, and of your foolish sentimentality! Ysar is dead, dead these hundred centuries! But you live—as I live— eternally! Let that reality sustain you! Now, do your duty, Commander!"

"He's telling the truth for once," Grayle said. "Ysar is dead, and only her undying machines—and a handful of immortal men—act out the dead dream."

"But—I remember Ysar . . ."

"Your memories are false," the *krill* said. "You were born aboard ship, Lokrien, nurtured in an amniotic tank, educated by cybertape! You were given the vision of that which once was and is no more, to inspire you in the performance of your duty. But surely now we can dispense with childish images! You live for your duty to Battle Command, as I do! Now, let me kill the traitor, and we will be on our way, once again to voyage outward, at home in the great emptiness of space!"

"Loki—it's bluffing! Without the coil, it dies—because that's what it draws its power from. That's why it came along—to keep an eye on the coil! Destroy it, and you destroy the ship—and its murderous robot with it!"

"Commander—perhaps I erred through overzealous-ness—but if you destroy the coil—you die too!"

"Do it now, Loki!"

"Fools!" the *krill* raged. "I tried to spare you the last, full knowledge of yourselves, but you leave me no choice. True, I am a construct of Xix, linked to the neural cir-cuitry of the ship, and with the death of the ship I die. But you, too, are constructs! Kill me, and you kill yourselves! Let me live, and yours is life eternal—even for the treacher, Gralgrathor!"

Grayle gave a short, harsh laugh. "If we're constructs, we're human constructs. We should be able to do what a man would do."

"I move swiftly, Lokrien—perhaps more swiftly than you think."

Falconer looked at the cat-thing, crouched, tail lashing, its eyes locked on him. He looked at Grayle, waiting, ignoring the terrible wounds across his chest.

"If I destroy the coil, we all die," he said softly, in English. "If I don't—the Earth dies."

"Decide, Commander," the *krill* said. "I will wait no longer."

11

Jess Dooley peered down into the gloom at the blurred figures below. He couldn't make out the details, just vague dark shapes against a deeper darkness. Until just now he hadn't had a clue as to what was going on; only that it was killing business. But he'd heard what the last fellow said, in plain American, about the Earth dying. That was plain enough. Everybody said World War Three wouldn't leave enough pieces to pick up for anybody to bother. Looked like the Russians were having words about—whatever it was they came here to do. One of them—the mean-voiced one—was for doing it right off. The other one, with the deep voice, was against it. And the third one wasn't sure. But he'd be making up his mind in a minute.

Jess got silently to his hand and knees. He wasn't sure yet just what it was he was going to do—but he knew that he'd have to do something, even if it was wrong. He blinked, trying to penetrate the blindness, trying to get a good look at the fellow with the dead man's voice. He was the one to watch, the one to stop. If he'd just move a little more this way. . . .

12

"For Ysar," Falconer said, and reached to close the contacts. The *krill* yowled in triumph, took two swift paces, reared above Grayle—

From the shadows above, a dark shape leaped, struck the cat-thing full across the back, unbalancing it enough that the stroke of its taloned paw went wide. It bucked, threw the man off, spun to leap at Falconer—

Fire burst from the hatch. In mid-spring, the cat-creature's body contorted. It struck the metal side of the machine, sprawled away from it, its limbs raking futilely in a last effort to reach Falconer, who sagged against the side of the unit, shaking his head dizzily. Grayle clung to the wall, fighting to stay on his feet.

"It lied . . . again," he whispered.

The *krill* lay limply; the light still glowed, but weakly, fading from the great eyes. It spoke in a dying voice:

"The long twilight . . . ends at last . . . in night."

13

"I'm all right, man," Dooley said as Falconer lifted him to his feet. "Don't tell me what that was I jumped; I don't want to know. Just get me out of this place."

"It's dead," Falconer said. "And the generators are stopping."

"But we're still alive," Grayle said. "That means we're bioconstructs, not mechanical. And now we're mortal creatures. We'll age and die like any man."

Falconer went to Anne, lifted her in his arms. "Until then we can live like any man."

They made their way up the echoing concrete steps, along the empty corridors. The first light of day gleamed beyond the shattered entrance. Already the wind was dying, the rain abating.

As the two men stepped out through the scattered rubble, light glinted on the dark hillside. Grayle leaped forward as a single shot rang out from the wooded slope above the building.

14

Captain Zwicky, coming up silently behind the man who lay in prone firing position behind the big pine, saw the stir of movement in the shattered entrance below, saw the two men step into view, heard the flat crack of the gun, threw himself on Harmon as he relaid his sights for the second shot.

"Why did you shoot him?" Zwicky shouted at the policeman as the latter wiped a big hand across his bloodied mouth. "Why?"

"Because," Harmon said with total conviction, "the son of a bitch thought he was better than I was."

15

"I'm sorry, brother," Falconer said. "Sorry for everything, but most of all for this."

"Xix was right." Grayle whispered. "But only half-right. Even the longest night . . . ends at dawn."

Carrying Anne, Falconer walked out across the dark lawn toward the waiting men.

(please turn page)

ROBERT A. HEINLEIN

GLORY ROAD	(N1809—95¢)
PODKAYNE OF MARS	(S1791—75¢)
STRANGER IN A STRANGE LAND	(Z1756—$1.25)
THE MOON IS A HARSH MISTRESS	(N1601—95¢)
STARSHIP TROOPERS	(S1560—75¢)
TOMORROW, THE STARS	(S1426—75¢)

    (edited by Robert A. Heinlein)

HARRY HARRISON

BEST SF: 1968	(S1742—75¢)

    (ed. by Harry Harrison and
    Brian W. Aldiss)

CAPTIVE UNIVERSE	(X1725—60¢)
THE TECHNICOLOR® TIME MACHINE	
	(X1640—60¢)
SF: AUTHOR'S CHOICE	(S1567—75¢)

    (ed. by Harry Harrison)

ARTHUR SELLINGS

THE POWER OF X	(X1801—60¢)
THE UNCENSORED MAN	(X1379—60¢)
THE QUY EFFECT	(X1350—60¢)

Send for a free list of all our books in print